I0457062

# MYSTERIOUS MERCHANDISE

A WITCH'S THRIFT SHOP MYSTERY BOOK 1

ASTORIA WRIGHT

NOVELWRIGHT
PRESS, LLC

Cover Art by freepik
http://www.freepik.com

Published by Novelwright Press, LLC
http://www.novelwright.com

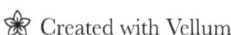 Created with Vellum

# A WITCHY NARRATOR

*I am a witch, but the heroine you will meet today is not. Her name is Alice, and to tell her story, I will have to turn back time to a year ago, on a rainy morning, when the leaves were turning, and the streets were drowning, and Alice Adelcraft was just walking into an unassuming store in the middle of Main Street. You will hear this tale through Alice's eyes, as I did through my crystal ball. And me? I will not appear until the very end of the last chapter, of the last book in what might be the last days of Alice's life. When I do, you'll likely be rooting for our heroine (quite rightly so), but I hope you will also be able to forgive me. And, more importantly, if I can make such a wish, so will Alice.*

# 1

## BLACK CATS AND RAINY DAYS

A bell dinged overhead. A gust of wind smacked the door shut as soon as it opened, plunging the knob into Alice Adelcraft's back. With an "Oof," Alice cracked a rib. That is, she snapped the rib of the umbrella she'd been fighting as she entered the shop. Dumping the drenched disaster into the bin by the door, Alice rubbed the sore spot where the doorknob had hit her spine.

Rain, sounding like Morse code from an old-timey war movie, beat down on the windows with the message that the storm would worsen still. Safe inside, Alice unwrapped her scarf and gave a mummy-worthy groan. The sound was fitting for the pitch darkness and the musty smell, reminiscent of an old, Egyptian tomb.

Not that Alice had been around in ancient times. Or to Egypt. She was half-Egyptian on her mother's side, English on her father's, and though her parents trekked the globe before finding each other, Alice, at twenty-eight, had seen no more of the world than the items in this room—which she couldn't see at the moment.

She bit at the wet gloves to pull them off her soggy fingers. Throwing the gloves onto a counter somewhere to her left, she waited for the *splosh* telling her she'd hit her mark. Then, she flicked the switch.

Lights on, the room became a blur of colors. Alice took off her rain-soaked glasses, reached over the counter for a tissue, and wiped the lens. Now the antique shop came into focus.

Many Treasures was a wonder, not a "Seven Wonders of the World" wonder, but a marvel nonetheless. Japanese and Chinese lanterns hung from the ceiling. Clocks ticked on the wall. Worn, but well-loved furniture held what were—for lack of a better word —*treasures:* paintings, books, money-boxes, maps, globes, compasses, and items only a scholar could identify.

The scholar who had founded Many Treasures, Eric Kinjo the First, Professor of Anthropology, died before Alice could meet him, but she imagined he had been a lot like her Egyptologist father. Both men came to Urbana for its World Cultures museum, Alice's father as a curator and Professor Kinjo as a collector generous enough to loan a rare artifact or two. And both men had died of heart attacks on the same day, as a matter of coincidence.

The professor's widow, Rin Kinjo, 64, currently owned the antique shop. But her true calling was telling the tales of her late husband's quests for the treasures they sold. Since Alice couldn't hear stories about her father, she relished the ones about the professor. In high school, Alice had listened on the edge of her seat—or rather, the stool behind the century-old cash register.

Alice's favorite tale involved a visit to the Middle East, where Professor Kinjo had studied jinn mythology. Mrs. Kinjo—with her flare for drama and her Okinawan accent, told the story like so:

"My husband's third day in Jordan, he met a man with a ring handed down through the generations of a wealthy, local family. The ring contained a jinn —you would call it a "genie" — who, if set free, would wreak havoc on the world. But the jinn was bested by a wizard and bound to the ring through a magical inscription, which enslaved the jinn to the ring's owner, to grant wishes for all eternity. Or so the man said before requesting 20 million rials—or 500 U.S. dollars—for the ring. I'd call that a bargain for unlimited wishes. But my husband was clever. He took a magnifying glass from his shirt pocket and read the sacred inscription. Though someone had tried to scratch them away, there were the words: "Made in China." The next day, my husband saw twenty of the same rings in a bazaar in Amman!"

By this point in the story, Professor Kinjo's grandson, Eric III, would say, "And then he found a real ring in Iran, but lost it to a sheik in a bet. Yes, Baa-Baa, we know the story."

"Our lives would be so different if we still had that ring," Mrs. Kinjo would say, her eyes straying to the family picture hanging on the wall by the register.

She meant the accident that had taken Eric's parents in his senior year of high school. Eric was always quick to change the subject, possibly because going from Eric

III, to Eric Jr., to the only Eric in short succession, was too painful to discuss. He'd offer his grandmother tea and lead her upstairs, her cane clicking the whole way up to their apartment.

Then Eric would jog back down the stairs, the same way he was clunking down the steps this morning, and say, as he was saying now, "I've got a ton of studying to do, Alice. The shop is yours."

Alice made the same quip as always, "Is that a promise, boss?" Then, she flipped the sign on the door to "Open." Sometimes, Eric would reply, "If it's in the stars," an infuriatingly cryptic message, borrowed from his late-father's favorite phrases. Other days, like today, all he gave her was a mumbled, "Mm-hmm."

Eric sat on the stool furthest from the cash register, his books sprawled out, and his nose buried. He wouldn't ring anyone up until he finished calculating and rechecking the equations in his Astrophysics text. That was likely to be a few hours, at which point Eric would lift his head, rub his neck, and say, "Need a break?" like he always did.

Well, she needed a break now.

Alice plonked her purse two inches from Eric's elbow. He glanced up and right back down, fixing his mind on an equation involving inertia and other natural forces. Alice had certainly faced a force of nature this morning.

Since her not-so-subtle gesture with the purse had gone unnoticed, Alice cleared her throat. "Eric. I know I'm wearing a black cardigan, so it's hard to tell, but I'm soaking wet. My purse is dripping, and my curls are frizzing like I've been flying a kite in a lightning storm."

He looked up, put a hand through his annoyingly luxurious, albeit short, hair and said, "Sorry. What happened?"

Alice pointed both hands to the window, game show host style. "It's raining, and a reckless driver splashed water all up the curb. I'm talking head-to-toe splash. I need a minute."

"Yeah, sure. Who would drive that fast down Main Street? Don't they know there's a police station right down the road?" As a grad student, Eric puzzled about the little things, fretted about the big things, and was working on the age lines that would one day show he had worried too much in his youth.

Alice might have been only a year older, but the school of life had crammed in a lot of lessons that year. It was testing her nerves today. She grabbed her purse and headed to the restroom.

Over her shoulder, she said, "I didn't see him coming. It was like he appeared right out of the alley just to splash me."

"That alley doesn't go through. There's no street there."

"I said it was *like* that. He must have swerved or something. I'd say he was drunk, but I wouldn't expect that from a limo driver."

Eric glanced out the storefront window. "A limo in this neighborhood?"

"There's one you see around from time to time if you'd look at anything but a textbook. Probably some rich guy and his chauffeur, who doesn't know how hard it is to get the damp out of these curls." Alice flipped light switch and turned in the doorway, adding, "I saw the passenger once, getting out of the car. He was a white man in a dark executive suit and one of those long, black coats. He had to be thirty or under, but he was holding something like a jeweled cane."

"And you thought he was handsome?"

"What? No. Why would you ask me that?" Even as Alice crossed her arms, she thought to herself that maybe he *was* handsome—in an 'evil villain' sort of way.

"You certainly remember lots of details about his appearance," Eric teased.

She did remember the entrancing blue eyes, the raven-black hair, the perfect posture. But the man was thin, and if he was muscular, it was in a lean sort of way…and…and why was she thinking about this?

She shook her head. "My point was about how rich he looked. How do you suppose you make that kind of money at our age?"

Eric, back at his books by now, responded absent-mindedly, "By not caring when you splash lowly sales-girls with muddy water on your way to success."

"Or not noticing them when they come into work drenched," Alice teased.

"I said I was sorry. You know what my grandmother would say: you're in a string of bad luck. But there's a meteor shower next week. You could wish for good luck then."

"Since when are you superstitious?" Alice asked.

"I'm not. You are. You're always talking about 'manifesting' your future with your vision boards and whatever. Didn't you go to a palm reader once?"

Alice straightened up tall, or as tall as her 5'3" frame allowed. "I'm not superstitious. I'm open-minded—there's a difference."

Eric replied, "All I'm saying is shooting stars are as good as anything else. Maybe it'll work this time—your self-fulfilling prophecy, I mean."

Alice's grip on the handle of the bathroom door tightened. "Keep watch for customers," she said, slamming the bathroom door behind her. *Self-fulfilling prophecies, indeed.*

An interview for an unpaid internship at the World Cultures Museum this afternoon had put Alice on edge. The unexpected shower on her way to work pushed her over into "bad mood" territory. She'd been so careful, staying away from the curb, using an umbrella, to no avail. Now she looked a mess.

Alice probably wouldn't get the position. The museum wasn't likely to accept a woman who had worked one semester and taken classes the next, on and off like that for eight years to get her Bachelor of Science in History. Her father's status wasn't likely to help, since he'd served as curator all of three weeks before passing away.

First impressions were everything. Alice had scheduled time between work and the interview to change, but not to redo her hair. Curls were a curse from the start, at least in Alice's case. Her hair was more frizz than curl on humid days, which were often in Urbana. And wet hair…forget it.

Alice plugged in the mini-blow-dryer she kept in the bathroom cabinet for these just-in-case days and tried to touch up the damp strands. Her dark-brown hair shined, and some might say she looked cute when she was finished. She wouldn't say it, but she appreciated those who did.

Alice saw herself as average in height and weight and everything. The rare compliment didn't change the facts: A brown-eyed beauty she was not. She accepted herself for what she was: a nobody.

She had dreams, but everyone had those in a rainy college town. A future is what Alice was missing. Or at least, hers wasn't going to manifest itself any time soon, no matter how many vision boards she taped to the wall of her one-bedroom rental in the Urbana Gardens apartment complex.

Eric and his grandmother didn't live in a space much larger than hers— she'd seen the upstairs apartment on holidays she'd spent with them—but she knew from keeping track of sales they had much more than they spent. Most of it would go to Eric's dream of becoming an astronaut. While his head was in outer space, hers was so down to Earth it hurt.

It literally hurt to tug at the knots as her hair fought to revert to its natural state. Between the brush, the blow dryer, and the leave-in conditioner, it was just starting to look interview-worthy when a crash came through the bathroom door. Brush still in her hand, Alice swung the door open and stuck her head out.

"What was that?" she asked a bewildered Eric.

"It's a…um." His jaw continued to open and shut, but his voice had left him.

Eric was staring at the back corner of the store, where the maps and books sat. A rustling noise came from that direction, prompting Alice to peer around the door. The sound stopped.

"Did something fall?" Alice asked.

Eric came around the counter, whispering, "Something came in from outside."

"What do you me—" The shuffling restarted. An old map, one in the form of a scroll, fell onto the floor, rolling to the tip of Alice's closed-toe flats. On the table, the kerfuffle stilled to a slow up and down movement. Something under the parchments was—breathing?

Instinctively holding the brush out like a weapon, Alice walked forward.

Eric put an arm in front of her. "What are you doing? Whatever it is might be rabid."

She pushed Eric's arm away gently and took two cautious steps. Alice could never control her curiosity. And she was fairly sure those were cat ears she saw poking out between the scrolls.

"Come on out, little buddy. We won't hurt you."

The maps shifted again. Two more scrolls fell to the floor. A pair of golden-yellow eyes followed the furry ears. Then a set of whiskers emerged.

"I wonder who the scaredy-cat is?" Alice looked back at Eric, grinning.

"Oh, very funny," said Eric. "I'm telling you something is wrong with that cat. It ran right through the door—*the closed door.*"

"Get your eyes checked, Eric. The wind probably threw the door open, and she ran in. Maybe the weather scared her. It's stormy out there, isn't it, kitty?"

"Alice, I'm telling you, an astronaut's eyes are better than 20/20. I know what I saw. That's not a normal cat. Don't touch it." He walked back to the counter and picked up the phone.

"Who are you calling?"

"Animal control."

Alice laughed, "Seriously?" She walked over to the cat and coaxed it gently, "Come here, kitty. That's a good girl." It walked into Alice's outstretched arms and nestled in between her elbows. "See? She's gentle. She even has a collar."

Doubt ran through Eric's brown eyes, but he put down the receiver. "What's the address on the collar?"

"Let's see." Alice flipped the gold, circular tag over, but the script was foreign-looking. *Arabic, maybe?* "There is no address. Oh, wait a sec." The lettering seemed to change before her eyes, which must have been a trick of the light. The light from the front counter was bright enough to make out the writing on the tag. Alice read the inscription aloud, "Hex? That's a strange name."

Eric sneezed. Holding a finger to his nose, he said, "Get that cat away from me."

"Mighty astronaut immune system. Looks like you're allergic. All right. Hold down the fort for a while. I'll go find Hex's owner."

"You sure you want to go out again in this weather?"

"No, but I still have my coat on and it's only drizzling now, so I'll brave it. Hex's owner can't be very far.

Back in a flash," she said. Lighting struck as if nature shared her sense of humor.

Thunder struck just as Alice, opened the door. Raindrops launching their assault on red bricks and asphalt. Alice lifted her hood and looked down the street. *Empty*.

Rubbing the cat's ear, Alice said, "Which way, Hex?"

As if she'd understood, Hex jumped down on the sidewalk. The way she turned her head to see if she was following gave Alice chills. Hex trotted with purpose to the alley between Many Treasures and the neighboring Thai restaurant.

There was nothing there but a dead end and a dumpster. If Hex's owner was hanging out here, Alice wasn't sure she wanted to meet him. Muggings weren't unheard of in the area.

Alice called over the rain, "I don't think your owner is behind the dumpster, Hex. Come on out."

She opened her mouth to laugh and left it hanging when she saw the wall behind the garbage disappear. An open road stood where the brick should have been. Many Treasures hadn't been on a corner the last time Alice checked. She backtracked around the front and back, just to be sure. And there it was: the sign reading Main Street and...

"Magic Row?" she read aloud.

As if on cue, the rain was gone. It might have stopped a minute ago. Alice wasn't sure how long she'd been gawking at the sign before the word registered in her brain. Clouds still cover the sky, threatening more harm to her hair.

The thought of her interview seemed silly now. A grin spread across her face. *A hidden street! How?*

Hex's ears twitched. The cat cocked her head as if waiting for Alice's shock to subside. A solid minute passed before Alice snapped back to reality, or whichever version of it she was in now. Hex nodded, then turned and continued forward.

"Wait," said Alice, moving expanded. "Where have you brought me, Hex?"

Alice would have thought it was an entirely different plane of existence, except that she could see Eric through the side window. The stores and restaurants behind her on Main Street all looked the same. Only now, there was an added row of shops blending in with the brick buildings all around. *How could she have missed an entire street?*

Alice walked deeper in—and nearly tripped. Regaining her balance, Alice looked down to see that her foot had caught on a ruby-red shoe. Not a shoe, it was a foot.

*Oh, please,* Alice thought to herself. *Please just be passed out. Please don't be—*

Dead. There was a woman behind the dumpster, lying cold on the ground. Alice always thought that people who saw dead bodies screamed loudly enough to cause the neighborhood to come running. The sound Alice made wasn't like that. Something between a shriek, a whimper, and a gag, escaped her lips. She stood there, frozen, while her brain decided between staring, screaming, and running away.

Staring won.

The woman had a shawl around her head, under which gray hairs were visible, along with a fair complexion and blue eyes. Those empty blue eyes stared lifelessly at Alice as if pleading for help. But she was beyond saving.

Alice's heart sank so deep into her gut, she thought she might throw up. Leaning on the dumpster, she retched. The stench of the trash wasn't helping. Alice pushed herself a few paces back to where she could breathe again.

Her foot caught a box, which she shook off. Then, seeing it was a package, she bent down to examine it. The "From" address was cut off, but there was still one word left on the "To" section. It read "Treasures" in unique, curvy and elegant handwriting, almost like calligraphy. *It had been sent to Many Treasures?* But Alice hadn't unpacked a box like this before.

Maybe "Treasures" was part of a street address or the name of an apartment complex. *Was this package the property of the woman?* Alice turned back to the sight. Mercifully, from this angle, she could only see the feet, which reminded her she'd just tripped over a corpse. She looked away, breathed deeply, and tried to regain her power of speech.

When she was able to use her voice again, she whispered, "Jeez, Hex. What have you gotten me into?"

## 2

## MAGIC ROW

"Is she dead?" A juvenile voice came from over Alice's shoulder.

The term "juvenile delinquent" came to mind when Alice saw the owner of the voice. There were two kids behind her when she turned around. The boy wore torn-knee jeans and a t-shirt that might have once been green. The girl barely filled in the jeans. The sweater, which sagged over her bony shoulders had to be a woman's hand-me-down. Both kids were blond-haired, brown-eyed, and fair-skinned. They looked like twin tweens if Alice was guessing.

Since the girl had asked the first question, the boy asked the next, "Did you kill her?"

Alice might have shot back with *"Did you?"* except these kids didn't look strong enough to hurt a fly, and Alice didn't want to give in to the stereotype adults placed on poor looking kids. In fact, she felt sorry now for thinking of them as delinquents.

Alice said, "No. The cat led me to her."

Alice bent down to get a closer look at the woman. Her face looked familiar, but not enough to name her. There was no purse and no visible ID, and Alice wasn't about to touch a corpse.

Looking at the kids, Alice asked, "Do either of you know her?"

The girl shrugged. "I've seen her around, but I don't know her name."

The boy said, "You don't know who you killed?"

Alice gave an *"I'm-not-amused"* look and re-examined the body. The kids leaned in, too. After a few uncomfortable seconds in which Alice realized the twins were staring at her. She said, "There's no cuts or bruises, so it's probably natural causes. No need to worry, you guys. I'll call to report it and you should get back to your parents, or to school or wherever you were going."

"Looks like a heart-stopping spell, but I'm not a healer," the girl said.

Alice ignored the use of the term "healer" instead of "doctor" and focused on the heart-stopping part. "You mean she had a heart attack?"

It wouldn't explain the look of terror on the woman's face. Alice had never seen such a mix of emotions on a dead person. The only bodies she'd ever seen were at the two funerals she'd attended in her life, and the morticians had made them look peaceful, like they were sleeping.

The girl leaned down and asked the cat, "Did you see the attacker?"

Alice swore Hex shook her head before jumping into the girl's arms.

The boy said to Alice, "You're new here, aren't you?"

What could she say? She still couldn't get over this pop-up street. "Here" was nowhere to Alice, and she had a feeling this nowhere was off-limits to people who stumbled into it by happenstance.

She answered cryptically, "Magic Row is new to me. How long has it been here?" She tried to sound nonchalant, but her voice raised at the end, betraying her high-strung emotions.

She sounded calm enough to fool the boy, who shrugged. "It's at least as old as us."

"We're fourteen," the girl volunteered.

*So, teens then, not tweens*, Alice noted. "What are your names?" she asked.

"I'm Hazel Willows. This is my brother Zade." Hazel reached out a hand while Zade stuck his in his pockets.

"Psst." Another kid, this one older—at least fifteen—with frazzled red hair, torn jeans and a long, blue, tunic-like shirt waved from around the corner of the closest store on their side of the street. "It's not safe to stay here."

Zade and Hazel didn't budge.

"Have you seen this?" Zade asked.

"Come on, or they'll think you did it," the boy said.

Across the road, a door flung open with enough force to grab Alice's attention. A brunette woman stood behind the glass door, looked up and down the row of shops, and shouted, "Hooligans!"

Zade and Hazel sprinted down the street, and

seemed to vanish before they reached the older boy. Alice watched in wonder as the Hispanic woman stepped onto the sidewalk. Cupping her hands around her mouth, the woman shouted, "I know you used magic to rattle my shelves, and if I catch you with any of my merchandise, you'll be hexed so your backside aches for a month!"

The boy grinned and disappeared behind the building. The saleswoman turned and walked back into the shop, the door closing behind her with a bang. Hex had disappeared somewhere, presumably following the teens. But Alice couldn't just go back to Many Treasures. She had to report the body.

Only, since this street never existed before, would it still exist after she called the police and asked them to investigate? Or would they come out here and find a wall and an empty space behind a dumpster, then scold her for wasting department resources? Doubting her senses, Alice looked around.

Magic Row didn't look too different than the surrounding neighborhood. This could have been any other street in Urbana: old brick buildings with brightly painted doors and tinted windows. The cars on the street were ordinary models. A man coming out of a shop lit a cigarette. The scene was normal enough— except that the name on shop he'd come out of read: Spellbinders. Alice's eyes drifted to the other stores: The Essential Mage, Reading & Co.: Bookstore and Future Readings, Familiars Pet Store. These shops could only belong to a street named Magic Row.

Did the people here really believe in hexes and

spells? Or was it some kind of joke? The woman across the street didn't seem to have a sense of humor. And unless it was a flat-out hallucination, the dead body had been real enough.

As angry as the shouting woman had been, she did look relatively normal, and so did the shop from which she'd come out. At least the store might have a telephone or know who to contact. Alice had left her cell in Many Treasures, but more than that, she had no idea to whom she was supposed to report a "death-by-spell."

Alice crossed the road.

Close up, the sign above the store read "A Witch's Thrift Shop." There had to be an inside joke here Alice wasn't getting. A smaller sign on the door read, "Shoplifters Will be Hexed."

One thing was becoming clear as a crystal ball: Alice wasn't in Urbana anymore. At least, not any part of the Urbana she knew. She opened the door. There was no bell alerting anyone to her arrival like there was in Many Treasures.

Instead of the stale scent of age-old maps, books, and used furniture, the pleasant scent of sage and lavender met Alice's nose. The place was well lit, blocking out the cloudy, dim day with its bright yellow hue. Rows upon rows of tall shelves and clothing racks greeted Alice.

In many ways, it might have been an ordinary thrift shop. But, upon inspection, the clothes were more like cloaks worn in Dracula movies, and the shelves were filled with items that looked like they belonged in a fantasy novel—wands included.

Aside from wands, there were silver, gold, and brass, Middle Eastern oil lamps on the shelves facing the window. The brass one seemed brighter than the others. At least, there was something about it that drew her closer. And it was inscribed on the side with an lettering similar to the script on Hex's collar. Alice couldn't help but reach for the lamp's handle.

"How can I help you?" the saleswoman, who looked far friendlier when she wasn't shouting, asked.

"How can I help you?" A voice drew Alice's attention away.

The saleswoman, who looked far friendlier when she wasn't shouting, wore a silver pin nametag that read, Celeste, and a smile that said she viewed Alice as a potential customer. That, in turn, reminded Alice she wasn't there to shop. She set down the lamp, though, she hadn't quite remembered picking up.

"Sorry, I, um, I'm here to, uh, do you have a phone?" Alice's sentence came out jumbled, but the point got through.

Celeste raised an eyebrow and gave a slow, deliberate, "Yes?"

The questioning tone made Alice feel she should explain. She honestly wanted to anyway. Though, she had a little trouble finding the words. "I—I found a— you see, there was a cat and, well, I wasn't expecting— but then this whole street was a surprise."

The higher Celeste's eyebrow went, the faster Alice spoke. She stopped herself, closed her eyes, took a breath, and tried again.

"There's a body in the alleyway across the street," she blurted out.

Alarm widened Celeste's amber eyes, and she beelined it to the window. From the storefront, all you could see were the ruby-red slip-ons. Celeste gasped and raised her voice.

"Vestra!" she called out to one of her employees. "Call Ron, now!" To Alice, she said, "Did you see who it was?"

"I don't know—a woman," Alice answered.

"Did she have one of those with her?" Celeste pointed at the shelf. Seeing Alice's confusion, Celeste clarified, "A lamp?"

Alice shook her head, "If she did, I didn't see it. Why?"

"Because if that is who I think it is, we have a monstrous problem on our hands."

## 3

## A TALENT FOR TROUBLE

"It's Daria Jinni, all right," the Black man in blue said. His uniform was that of every other Urbana officer. He was striking in that he was possibly the most handsome man Alice had ever met. Six-foot something and stretching the cloth of his shirt just enough to see muscles bulging beneath, Office Oberon Knight took out a sketchpad and began asking questions.

"You're the one who found her?"

"*Yes, I am, Officer Knight,* Alice said confidently in her mind. In her throat, the words caught. When they finally made it out of her lips, the proverbial frog in her throat seemed to be the one who answered. It croaked out, "Ya, mmm, Sir Knight, mister, I mean...officer."

Officer Knight's brows furled sympathetically. He let go of the notepad and put a hand on her shoulder. She felt a spark at the touch, but the real magic was in the hovering notepad. The pen—also floating—scribed something onto the paper as the officer spoke.

"I can imagine how you feel. If you need to sit

down, I'm sure Celeste is fine with us using her office. And there's no need to call me anything formal. Fair Maidens may always call me Ron."

*Is he playing good cop?* Alice asked herself, as her mouth hung open. Partly, she had expected a hard-nosed officer to come in through the door behind him and start drilling her on what she'd seen. *Just the facts, ma'am.* Partly, she'd expected the officer to tell her she'd imagined the whole thing. But no part of her expected a wizard police officer, much less one with the Urbana PD.

*Was her heart beating so fast because of the revelation, the magical notepad, or his hand on her shoulder?* He let go, taking the paper back into his hands as if there was nothing special about the notepad or the embrace. Officer Knight—Ron—asked Alice something. She shook her head, then felt Celeste's hand patting her back.

"Are you all right?" Celeste asked.

"I'm fine." Alice's heart beat returned to normal. She pushed her glasses up the bridge of her nose. Now she could process Ron's question. "And, uh, Alice, that's my name."

Ron smiled, and Alice felt dizzy. Yes, he had a chiseled jaw, but no, it wasn't his looks. It was shock. Alice was still reeling from the events of the day. And now she felt nauseas. She reached a hand out and leaned on the shelf, trying to make it look casual. No need for this *Knight* to know she was trying not to throw up on his shining badge.

"Can you describe how you came upon Ms. Jinni?" Ron asked.

Clearing the pesky frog in her throat, Alice answered, "The cat, Hex, led me to her."

It sounded like a question. *I am questioning my sanity,* Alice thought. She took a breath, hoping he wouldn't think she was crazy as she described the whole situation from Hex, the cat, to Zade and Hazel Willows.

Her words were less jumbled than when she'd tried to explain to Celeste. They would have been clearer if not for Ron's green eyes boring into her. Darn him for being so charming. Darn her glasses for insisting on sliding down her nose every five seconds.

"Did you see anything suspicious before finding the body?"

Alice wanted to reply, *"Yeah, an entire street hidden by magic."* That wouldn't be unusual to a witch or a wizard officer—*was she accepting that as true now?*—but what would such be considered out of the ordinary in the magical community? Probably the non-witch who had stumbled into their street.

Alice shook her head, then realizing her hair was still damp from the speeding limo, she said. "Wait. Yes, I did see something. There was a car, a black limousine, that came out of nowhere—I mean, I think it turned the corner off of Magic Row and went speeding past the shop where I work."

"The shop you described, that's the antique shop, isn't it? I didn't know that was one of ours," Ron said.

Alice found herself nodding, not realizing he was accusing her of something until Celeste moved between her and Ron. "Our people go in there all the time. You can stop pointing fingers at good Samaritans. She didn't have to report it, you know."

With her hands on her hips, Celeste insisted Many Treasures was a magical establishment. *Why?* Alice realized working right outside of Magic Row might be a dead giveaway she was just a regular person who got too close to whatever this place was. *"Magic"* came to mind, and she considered. *Was this a street hidden by magic? Did other non-magical people stumble into this street once in a while? If so, what happened to them?*

Ron flipped his notebook shut and held up his hands, relenting. "My apologies. I know that was difficult for you, Alice, and I'm grateful for your assistance. I don't think I'll need to bother you again, but just in case…" He handed the notebook to her.

"Oh, sure," Alice said, realizing what he was asking. She was a little surprised an officer would hand her his notebook like that but flipping it open, she didn't see any notes scrawled inside. *Disappearing ink? Or did the words he jotted here somehow magically end up in his computer at the precinct?* Taking the pen Ron was offering, Alice wrote her name, address, and phone number on the first page.

"Thank you." Ron took the notebook.

"I just hope I was helpful," Alice replied.

"You were. In fact, I'm sure I have enough to go off of given your statements. Now, I've got a couple trouble-makers to talk to, if you ladies will excuse me."

"Remember that they're only children, Ron." Celeste's bottom lip dipped. Despite her yelling at them earlier, she seemed to have a soft-spot for Hazel and Zade, assuming that's who Ron had meant.

"I won't forget that, but you also can't forget they nearly burned down your shop last week," Ron said, opening the door.

"That was an accident," Celeste replied.

Ron shook his head, seeming rueful as he said, "Maybe this was, too." Then he walked through the door and disappeared from sight—not as in *stepped out of view*. He *disappeared.*

Alice knew she was out of her depth here, but she had to ask, "He doesn't think those two kids killed that woman, does he?"

Celeste sighed and walked with Alice to the back counter of the store. "The Willow kids have been causing trouble since their mother moved them here. They're Talented and untrained, and that is a dangerous combination." Celeste lowered her voice and looked at her with a strange smile. "But then, being Untalented yourself, you wouldn't know anything about that, would you?"

"I—" Alice shook her head. She may have just been insulted, or she was missing something. Guessing the latter, she admitted, "I don't know what you mean."

Celeste whispered, "You're not a witch, are you?"

Alice felt worse than the frog-in-your-throat feeling she'd had with Ron. Now, she felt like the frog itself, having recently been transformed by a witch. *Was Celeste a witch? Was she going to turn Alice into something terrible? Is that what had happened to Hex?*

Thoughts zoomed through her brain at dizzying speeds until one stuck in her mind. If Celeste had wanted to out her for not being a witch, she wouldn't have stuck up for her with Ron. She didn't want to harm Alice.

Slowly, Alice nodded.

Celeste said, "I suspected as much. Though, with a name like Adelcraft, I couldn't be sure you weren't one of us."

"Who is 'us?'"

"Witches and Wizards: those with magical talents, whether it's to see the future, cast spells, manipulate perception, or change reality itself. It's always the ones with strange abilities that are cast out of your society and into ours. Talents run in families, so I can usually tell the magical talent from the last name. It's a hobby of mine: Onomastics, the study of names. But more and more people are marrying out of the magic community, and it isn't a large community in Urbana to begin with, so my hobby isn't too useful here."

"And you recognize 'Adelcraft?'"

"Only the 'craft' part—it usually refers to magic, but I don't recognize the full name. I'd have to consult my books. You haven't noticed any magical talents in yourself, have you?"

"Not the magical kind. I like to think I have some other skills, though," Alice said, though none came to mind.

"Naturally. We don't mean it as an insult, you know. Well, it might be a little jab if we're honest, since your kind used to burn us at the stake and all. You can see why we wouldn't want one of you on our street."

"I'll try not to take it personally."

"Oh, I didn't mean to offend. I really don't have

anything against the Untalented. We can't self-sustain in our own communities anyway, so we interact with your kind every day. Some of us share in your achievements, too." She pulled out a smartphone and winked, then slipped it back into her pocket. "And anyway, it's Hex's job to keep your kind out, so if she let you in, we should probably be glad you're here. Still, Untalented people aren't supposed to be on Magic Row. If the rest of the witches and wizards here find out what you are…"

"They'd drive me out. I get it."

"No, I'm afraid you don't. They would hex your memory, Alice."

"So, I wouldn't remember Magic Row?" she asked, debating whether the memory of a dead body was one she wanted to keep anyway.

"The Mage Establishment, *mage* being the collective word for members of the magic community – witches and wizards alike, don't take chances. Depending on who casts it, the spell will likely be one that wipes your memory clean. You might not even remember who you are."

Alice gulped. "I think I'd better get back to the shop."

"Good idea. And Alice?" Celeste asked.

"Yeah?"

"Take care of yourself. I wasn't joking when I said Daria's death was a problem for all of us. It might be for you, too. Keep an eye open for trouble."

## 4

## WITCHY CUSTOMERS

Several strange customers had come into Many Treasures antique shop over the years. Some donned long capes, some wore jewelry reminding Alice of a gypsy stereotype, and some had simply said things that made no sense. One had asked if they sold ancient talismans, for instance, which wasn't so weird in itself, except they tacked on: "And do you know if they're still active?"

Since magic wasn't real before this morning—to Alice at least—she thought it an utterly ridiculous question. Now, she wasn't so sure. Unless she'd hit her head chasing the cat down the alleyway and dreamed the entire thing up, *she'd met actual witches and wizards* today. *Hadn't she?*

Through the course of the day, she'd touched her head three times, feeling for a bump that wasn't there. Once, she'd asked Eric if a cat really had come into the store. It had. Twice, she'd squinted suspiciously at odd-looking customers, wondering if they were actually witches. *Did they think she was one, too?*

Many Treasures was on the corner of Magic Row, and not in the middle of Main street as she'd thought before. *Did that mean witches and wizards wandered in here from time to time? Did they see the unusual trinkets and assume they were magical? Or were they magical, as Mr. Kinjo had hoped when he'd first begun collecting them?*

Alice looked at the objects with new understanding. Her eye specifically caught on the maps and books where Hex had hidden earlier. A glint of gold drew her to the stack of scrolls. Shifting them aside, she found an oil lamp so similar to the ones in Celeste's store, she wondered if it hadn't been one of the ones from A Witch's Thrift Shop. Alice picked the lamp up by the handle. *Had the twins or that mysterious boy stolen this? Had Hex been their accomplice?*

Maybe it hadn't come from Celete's store. Ron had confirmed that Daria Jinni had been murdered and Celeste had asked her if Daria had been carrying a lamp? *Was this Daria's lamp?* And, more importantly, *had she been murdered for it?*

That very thought rang through her mind as the bell above the door resounded. Alice turned to greet the customer, saw the woman's black fur cloak, and, for some reason she didn't fully understand, hid the lamp back under the scrolls. Placing a smile on her face, Alice walked to the front counter.

"Good morning! Welcome to Many Treasures. Are you looking for anything in particular?" Alice asked.

The woman's dark eyes traveled over Alice, sizing

her up. Alice instantly disliked her when she smirked with an air of superiority. The woman's overdressed 1920's style clothing gave her villainous vibes, complete with the pointed nose and the single gray streak in her long, wavy black hair.

In a slight Farsi accent, which Alice only recognized because she'd had a Persian neighbor, the woman said, "I am looking for an oil lamp. Gold, if you have it."

That cinched it. Alice was ready to call the police and report her on suspicion of being…suspicious. She had to remind herself she wasn't even sure Hex had brought in the lamp. Mrs. Kinjo might have recently added it to the collection. Maybe it had come in the box…the one beside the deceased Mrs. Jinni. If it was related to Daria's death, then it would be folly not to hand it over to the police, and it seemed sketchy that anyone should be asking for it.

Fake smiling, Alice replied, "Sorry, we don't carry those." Then, because she had this wild streak in her she had never quite learned to control, she added, "You could try around the corner and across the street."

The woman quirked her head and met Alice's eyes. The smirk became a genuine smile. Perhaps this woman reserved the air of superiority for the Untalented alone.

"I will. Thank you. If you do come across a lamp, please contact me." She handed Alice a card.

It was a normal-looking business card reading "Qadira Cassel" and describing her occupation as an architect. Her catchphrase was unique: *Don't get rooked. Build your castle with Cassel.*

"You build castles?" Alice asked. "Mansions are the modern-day castles, aren't they?" Qadira said.

"True, I guess. But in Urbana?" Alice's surprise was genuine. Urbana didn't boast many mansions, except maybe up the hill on Enchanted Avenue. The name was just hitting her now for what it really meant.

"Please, call me Qadira." She'd mastered politeness in minutes. "I have a customer just outside the city. He owns property here. Perhaps you've heard of Sebastian Delvaux?"

That was another villainous name if Alice had ever heard one. Maybe he was using Qadira to fetch the lamp he'd killed to get. *Stop*, Alice reprimanded herself, *you can't accuse people you know nothing about of murder.*

Alice shrugged, trying not to be suspicious of everyone, "I can't say I've heard of him."

Qadira raised an eyebrow. It was her turn to look at Alice suspiciously. Alice blushed, which was thankfully hard to notice on her warm-toned skin, and wondered what she'd said wrong. *Was Sebastian someone whom a witch was supposed to know? Why?*

If he was building a mansion, he was rich, for one. He might be a prominent member of the magical community. Alice debated for a second feigning forgetfulness.

She could say, "Oh, *that* Sebastian Delvaux. Yes, of course. How could I not know him? Everyone does!"

But before she could open her mouth again, Qadira said, "Well, thank you, Miss—?"

"Alice." She figured it might be best not to give her last name—just to be on the safe side.

"Alice, please call me if a lamp turns up. It may be a matter of police interest."

"Oh?" Alice asked. If Qadira was a murderer, it was bold of her to admit that she was interfering with a police investigation.

"I don't want to say too much, but the lamp needs protecting—our kind of protection, if you catch my drift —and it ought to be returned to its owner before anyone can do damage with it."

"Rightful owner? Was it stolen?" Alice asked.

"Centuries ago—but not recently. Its owner was killed, so it needs another, and there's only one candidate in town who can handle that particular lamp."

"Who is that?"

"Me," Qadira said, slipping a pair of black shades over her eyes. With that last word, she gave a parting smile and walked out the door.

The bell's chime was the start of a headache for Alice, and the rest of the day became a migraine-induced blur. She hid the lamp in her purse straight away. Next, Alice called the museum saying something had come up and, thankfully, they were able to reschedule her interview. Alice's hair was beyond saving anyway. She took the lamp around the corner and was dismayed to see that Magic Row, despite her best efforts to find it, was no longer there.

## 5

## THE GENIE IN THE LAMP

Home was a cramped and dreary space, but it was a great relief after the day she'd had. Before anything else, Alice dropped her bag onto the coffee table and sank into the sofa. She sighed, relieved today was over.

The migraine jumbled all her thoughts so she was half-convinced she'd made up half of the day's events and misinterpreted the rest. Some other time, when her head wasn't throbbing like someone had hexed her brain with a pain spell—that had to be a thing—she would try to sort out fact from fantasy.

At the moment, she laid her head on a sofa pillow and rubbed her temples, wanting nothing more than to drift off to sleep. Except—*how could she sleep with the question of her sanity looming in the air?* Her eyes moved to the lamp, sticking out of her purse.

*What would it hurt to stop rubbing her temples for a second and give the lamp a try?* If magic was real, she'd rub the lamp, a genie would appear, and she'd wish away the headache—and any future migraine-causing catastrophes. If magic wasn't real, which is what Alice had believed until today, then after she touched the lamp, she'd call it a day and go to bed. Sure, Alice would fall asleep dreaming of black cats and golden lamps, but the world would make sense again in the morning. And if it didn't, she could always get a cat-scan.

Taking the oil lamp out of her purse, Alice set it on the table. She rubbed her own hands together first, as if preparing for a delicate procedure, took a breath, and placed a palm on the side of the lamp. It was cool to the touch.

"Here goes nothing," Alice said aloud.

Her palm warmed the surface, but after a good ten seconds of rubbing, that was all that happened. Alice laughed. She wasn't sure if that was the outcome for which she was hoping, but in a way, she did feel relieved. She shook her head at her own silliness, then froze.

Her eyes locked with a stranger standing in the corner of her apartment. She didn't get a clear look at him since he was standing in the shadows but caught enough to know he was a large man. An oversized, muscular home-invader stared at her with who knows what intentions.

Alice jumped over the back of the sofa with more agility than she knew she possessed. Her pounding headache became the pulsing of a fast-paced heart, her blood pumping her legs into action. She didn't stop until she was around the kitchen counter and ducked down. Over her heartbeat, her ears were keen enough to hear the creaking of the floorboards as the intruder took steps forward.

"Hello?" a masculine voice asked.

Alice closed her eyes and prayed silently before reaching a hand over the counter. She'd left a knife out after cutting her apple this morning. It had to still be there.

"Please, please, please," she whispered.

"I can see your fingers," the man said, more like a confused statement than a threat. Still, he was a strange man in her apartment, and she wasn't going to stand up unarmed. Finally, her fingertips found the serrated-blade. She grabbed for the handle and stood.

Holding the blade outward, she asked, "Who are you, and what do you want from me?"

He squinted and looked around. Walking forward, he asked, "Where's Daria?"

As he approached, Alice plunged the knife forward, shrieking, "I'm warning you!"

The man appeared behind the counter in a flash. He grabbed her wrist, twisting gently yet forcefully enough to make the weapon drop. Metal clanged sharply as it skidded from tile to carpet.

"Who are you fighting, human?" The man asked.

"You!" She wriggled to no avail.

The man, still clamping her arm in his massive fingers, scanned the room. "Are you the only human here?" His grip loosened.

Alice pushed him away, yelling, "Ow! Stay back!"

He sank to one knee. His turbaned head lowered.

Still panting, Alice cradled her wrist and squinted at

the large man who was…*bowing at her?* She grabbed the knife off the ground and held it up. Taking her phone out of her purse while holding the knife toward the intruder, Alice dialed 911.

The man stayed on the ground as the phone rang. Alice eyed him. The puffy, celestial blue pants, the gold vest, the gold bracelets, and the goatee all looked like something out of a storybook. The phone rang a second time.

"How long are you going to make me stay like this, mistress?" The man growled through clenched teeth.

It dawned on Alice. This man had appeared after she'd rubbed the lamp. There was no other explanation than the one her aching brain was telling her had to be true.

"911, What's your emergency?"

Alice's mouth opened, but nothing came out. *What would she say?*

*Hi, there's a burly, Arabic man in my apartment. I'm pretty sure he's a genie. Why? Because he came out of an oil lamp that a black cat brought me after a witch was murdered on a hidden street called Magic Row.*

The dispatcher would crack jokes about how there are no laws against making wishes. Or he'd say he couldn't put an APB out for a witch hunter. That is if he didn't send an officer over ASAP with a straight-jacket.

"Hello? Are you there?" The dispatcher asked.

Alice could prove she wasn't crazy. After all, she'd spoken to a police officer today. She gave a full testimony after she found a body.

"Wrong number, sorry!" Alice clicked off the phone.

Lowering the knife, she took a half-step toward the man. "Who are you?"

The man said, "Naveed of Amman."

That wasn't enough information. He was Jordanian and his name was Naveed. What would she do with that? His skin was a blueish-gray, his eyes unnervingly black, and his sheer size would make him stick out of any crowd like a sore thumb. He couldn't just be an intruder.

"OK, Naveed. Where did you come from?"

"I was born of air and fire."

"No, no, just now. Where did you come from just now? Why are you in my apartment?"

"I suppose you bought my lamp. Whatever you paid was a bargain."

Suspicions confirmed. Only it was impossible. Alice struggled to put the revelation into words. "Are you saying you came out of the lamp? Like a…like a…"

Naveed looked up. His eyes shone like polished obsidian. Or it might have been the tension in his exposed muscles that made Alice suddenly feel off-balance.

"Are you saying you do not know what you purchased?" Naveed stood. "Are you or are you not a witch?"

Alice pointed the knife higher, "I'm– that's not the question here. Are *you* a—" She found it hard to breathe.

"A jinn. The word you're looking for is a jinn. Or genie, as you Americans say." He stepped forward.

"I warned you to stay back!"

Naveed stopped, uttering something in a foreign language. He ran a hand through his hair and said, "Of all the possible buyers, Daria had to give me to an Untalented human."

"You know about the Talented and Untalented… thing?" Alice asked.

Naveed slid forward, unnaturally, so that he was in her face, yet far enough she was sure he was still obeying her order. He lifted a finger and her chin lifted with it, though he didn't touch her. Her cheek turned one way, then the other, then together. Through pinched cheeks, Alice's voice wavered, "I freed you. You have to listen to me. I told you to stay back, that includes no magical…funny business."

Naveed dropped his hold on her. "If you are Untalented, you lack not only magic, but the knowledge to control me. I am from one of the most powerful tribes of jinn and you know nothing about me. I can use that against you, and believe me, I will." He laughed.

Alice racked her brain. Her heart raced, but she tried to make herself look stern. She set the knife down on the counter.

"I do know you. You were grounded to the human world through a lamp, so you're a fire jinn. Powerful? Yes. But not half as powerful as a jinn of the air, who would be grounded by objects that carry emotions, like a ring."

"More powerful than me." Naveed scoffed, "That's debatable."

"And the form you're in now is your true appearance, close to human but not quite, which tells me you're unpracticed. A more experienced jinn could change shape to blend in."

"Wrong. I would never choose to look human. And this is not my natural form. I am a giant. I could outsize this building and crush you if I wanted." He grew a head taller and laughed just to make the point.

Alice held her head high, keeping a firm voice as she said, "Yes, Naveed, you've shrunk yourself to my size. Your pride is still bigger than your power. I am master of your lamp, after all."

The laughter died on his lips. He asked, more seriously this time, "Are you a witch or not?"

"Does it matter? I freed you."

"But you cannot hold me," he said.

"Oh, yes, I can. I know the rules." Alice was trying very hard to remember Mrs. Kinjo's stories, but she wouldn't let him catch on to that. She said confidently, "Those bracelets are a bond between you and the lamp, my rubbing that lamp was like signing a contract." Good. So far, she remembered. But there was something else, something about names. She hoped she'd remember as she spoke.

"Naveed, you told me your name because you thought I was a witch and would get it out of you anyway, but names carry power when it comes to jinn magic. When you told me your name, you gave me that power over you. If I even *think* of your name, any request I give you is an order. You're compelled to listen, and to respond honestly if I have any questions about your magic. Sound about right?"

Naveed glowered, but relented. "What questions do you have?"

She almost retorted that she had no questions because she knew everything she needed to know about jinn. But the truth was that she didn't know any more than Mrs. Kinjo had told her, and she didn't even know where to begin when it came to questions. An "um" escaped her lips involuntarily.

Naveed smirked, "See? You don't know. You can't truly control me if you're not a witch."

*Was that true?* Alice almost panicked. But she'd already controlled him by telling him to stay back. If she really had no power over him, wouldn't he be attacking instead of talking?

Alice said, "The wizard who imprisoned you used *your* magic as the contract. The terms don't require *me* to use *my magic* to control you." She hoped that was right. Plus, she hoped he fell for the notion that she might have magic of her own.

Naveed crossed his arms in classic manly-man—or jinnly-jinn?—style. "You're clever, for an Untalented human. But, jinn are not so easily controlled. You need knowledge and power to be the master of my lamp."

So much for that. They could keep bantering all day —both were perceptive enough to know the other was bluffing. If Naveed had known Alice at all, he'd have realized that intimidation fueled the rebellious streak in her.

It was time to show who was boss. Alice really, *really* hoped that was her. If not, she might not live long enough to regret it.

She took a breath. She thought of Naveed's name until it almost became a picture in her mind, like text on a page. Once she had it, she pointed at the glittering, gold jinn-prison atop the coffee table. "Magic or none, I can put you back into that lamp with one word."

Naveed uncrossed his arms, his face a mix of shock and anger. "You won't have time to—"

"Return!"

"Dammi—" The word was cut off by the curse of Naveed's imprisonment.

## 6

## BACK TO THE SCENE OF THE CRIME

T he next day, despite it being her day off from work, Alice woke early. She still had a mild aching in her temples, but the real pain on her mind was the big-blue pain in the neck currently trapped in the oil-lamp. She paced back and forth in her apartment, glancing at the lamp every five steps.

She could take the lamp to a police station. *Did Officer Knight work at the local precinct?* Maybe she could request to hand it to him directly. Then again, he might start asking her questions. The more she interacted with a wizard police officer, the more likely it was he would realize she wasn't a witch.

Her hundredth time pacing, Alice stopped and picked up the lamp. There was only one choice. She had to go back to A Witch's Thrift Shop and give the lamp to Celeste. Naveed had assumed she bought hims, so that might have been where Daria Jinni had intended to take the lamp in the first place. The only problem was she would need help getting back onto the street.

Alice stopped pacing and put the lamp on the kitchen counter. She could stuff it in a cabinet behind the dishes and leave it there forever. Or until the killer came for it and she faced the same fate as the previous holder of the lamp. The thought propelled her hand.

Alice pulled back, not afraid to rub the lamp, but realizing there was a better way. She knew now that she *did* have control of the jinn. The few facts Mrs. Kinjo had shared were right. One was that she could summon a jinn without touching the object to which he was bound.

"Naveed, you may appear." Alice felt a little silly when nothing happened.

Then a deep voice from behind her asked, "What is your wish?"

Alice spun on her heels to see Naveed materializing on the sofa chair across from her. He kept his head turned to the side, and his chin lifted snootily in the air.

Choosing calm over cardiac arrest, Alice put a hand on her hip instead of over her heart. She was proud of herself for not screaming, even more delighted she could respond with a nonchalant sarcasm. "Are you really not going to look at me?"

Naveed shifted his black eyes to glare at Alice. "I must serve you. I do not have to like it."

He was still muscular and gray-skinned and alarming to the eye, but scary? Not to Alice, not anymore. She took a seat on the couch and softened her expression, saying, "I think we should start over. My name is Alice."

Naveed raised a hand as if commanding silence,

"You are an unfortunate stop on the way to the next witch who steals me from you because you do not have the power to keep a real witch from me."

"You're right: I'm not a witch. I'm just an Untalented human who happens to know about jinn."

"You do not know everything—most humans do not. And now that I know you are not a witch, you best believe I will find the holes in your knowledge and use them to break free of you."

"Is that what you did with Daria?"

"She sold me, no doubt, to that odorous thrift shop she's always threatening to put me in. Though how an Untalented found her way into that place—"

"I didn't find your lamp at the thrift shop. I work at an antique shop that specializes in rare artifacts."

This caught his interest, "Antique shop! Why would Daria take me there?"

"Your lamp was brought to me, but not by Daria. She's dead."

"Dead?" Naveed's mouth dropped. For the first time, he seemed to possess emotions other than anger. Like... *sorrow?*

"I'm sorry, Naveed." Alice was sorry that she'd said it so bluntly. She had expected him not to care.

He stiffened. "Why? One master is the same as any other. It doesn't matter to me." Red lines formed around the black in his eyes, proving quite the opposite was true.

Alice gave him what little reassurance she could, "The police are looking into it. If it was murder, I'm sure they'll find out who killed her."

"Perhaps I killed her." Naveed's threatening smile

broke in seconds. He could only manage being half-heartedly menacing.

Alice was getting used to his temperament. She'd seen people like him before. He wasn't an egomaniacal bully. It just made him feel better to act like one.

"Look, Naveed, like it or not, you and I are stuck together—at least for a little while. You can't scare me or intimidate me, but if you want to part ways with me, all you have to do is help me get you back to Magic Row."

Naveed popped out of his chair and whooshed to the door with preternatural speed. "Is that all?" he asked, opening the door and gesturing with his hand, as if he were a gentleman saying *"After you."*

"Wait." Alice stood and held out a palm. "There are people out there looking for you, and I have no idea if they're friend or foe. Have you heard of a woman named Qadira Cassel?"

Naveed shrugged, "No, but then I don't pay much attention to human names. What little power human names have, I can't use them over any of you as long as I wear these." He pointed to his bracelets, which Alice thanked God were secured to his wrists. She wasn't sure what he meant by human names having power, but she was sure she didn't want to find out. She preferred not to dwell on the subject.

"All right, so I don't know if she's involved in Daria's death or not, but I'd rather she not see you until I'm sure. Can you transform into something? Like a normal person?"

"Normal? You mean human. No, thank you."

"Would you prefer to be an animal?"

He glared as he transformed from head to tail into a black alley cat similar to Hex. The dark eyes were the only part of him that stayed the same in feline form, and the way they were shooting daggers at Alice made her spine tingle. *Show no weakness*, she reminded herself. Alice crossed her arms.

"You'd really rather be a cat?"

Naveed meowed in answer and trotted out the door. Grabbing her jacket, purse, and the lamp, Alice followed him out of the Urbana Gardens Apartments and down the street. She had to hurry to keep pace, which made it difficult to tuck the lamp out of sight in her bag.

"Slow down!" Alice half-whispered, half-yelled.

Naveed's only response was turn and hiss at her, then continue on his way. The pause had been enough for her to catch up. She had enough time to zip the purse closed, too. And now that the lamp was hidden, Alice looked around, hoping no one had seen it in the first place.

The weather was still damp, and it took enough attention to avoid the puddles on the cracking sidewalk. In the early morning hours, the red brick buildings of Main Street were lit by old-fashioned lamplights. They had their own charm, but cast strange shadows on the walls. The atmosphere was eerie in the alley by Many Treasures.

When she first turned the corner, she was met with the usual sight. A dumpster by the brick wall and a short alleyway ending in nothing—it was just a gap between Many Treasures and the next store on Main Street. But when Naveed passed the dumpster, he disappeared straight into the wall.

"Naveed!" Alice whispered. She circled the dumpster. The cat-jinn was nowhere in sight. "Great," she muttered to herself.

She was alone in "death alley," as she was now thinking of it, staring at a dead end. Naveed had abandoned her! Alice supposed that was one way of solving the problem. She could turn around, walk into Many Treasures and forget all about Naveed, the cat-jinn. Except she still had his lamp. Alice looked up and down the street, then entered the alley. She walked to the back wall, looking for a door or something that would let her in.

Seeing nothing, Alice recalled Eric's exclamation about Hex yesterday, that the cat had gone *"right through the door."* And just now, Naveed seemed to go right through the wall. She wondered.

Putting a cautious palm against the red brick, Alice pushed. With the slightest pressure, her hand, then her leg, then her whole body went through the wall and emerged on the other side. Once again, Alice found herself standing on the corner of Main Street and Magic Row.

Naveed, glancing over his shoulder as if to say *"took you long enough,"* shook his furry head, and trotted across the street. Alice didn't care if he thought she was slow. Magic was new to her, and if she wanted to marvel a minute, open-mouthed and gaping like a fish out of water, that's just what she would do.

Eventually, Alice regained enough composure to

follow Naveed to A Witch's Thrift Shop. The store wasn't open yet, but Alice could see movement in the window. She knocked on the glass and waved.

Inside, Celeste gasped, stomped to the door, and greeted Alice with, "What, by the stars, are you doing here? Has Hex brought you again?" Celeste knelt down to pet "Hex," then titled her head curiously at the black-eyed cat glaring back at her.

"May I come in?" Alice asked.

Standing up, Celeste said, "I think you'd better. And tell me who I was just petting, and if it is who I think it is, why you would do something so foolish as to bring him back here."

## 7

## A WITCH'S THRIFT SHOP

"I didn't know where else to go, so I thought it best to come to you," Alice said at the end of her explanation. The back office of A Witch's Thrift shop had a small coffee pot. It was not a witch's device, but what it brewed was pure magic to Alice's overwrought nerves. Naveed refused to transform out of cat form and be helpful.

Instead, he'd walked straight to the newcomer in the room. Celeste's early-bird employee—Vestra, by her nametag— was a curvy woman with long hair so blonde it was practically white and clothes that clung tightly to her hourglass figure. She didn't seem to notice Naveed was a jinn and pampered him with cookies and a back rub.

Vestra stroked Naveed's fur, remarking, "What an adorable cat! I don't see a collar. What's his name?"

Naveed looked at Alice with his brow raised. Alice's lips turned devilishly upwards as a name popped into her head, "Fluffy. Fluffy McScratchins."

Naveed hissed. Vestra picked him up, held him against her considerable bosom, and cooed, "Oh, it's OK, Fluffy. I'm a friend, see?" She held a hand out to Alice, "Vestra Elstar, Celeste's *star* employee."

"Alice Adel—"

"You have some new inventory to sort through by the counter, better get on that before we open," Celeste said.

Vestra protested,"It's way too much stuff to sort through on my own."

"Get Mara to help you," Celeste said.

"She's not here."

"Yes, I am." A young woman appeared in the doorway, tucking her purple hair behind her ears. Her eyes were almost the same shade, a grayish blue bordering on lavender. Strange as she looked, she was also incredibly familiar.

"I know you, right?" Alice asked. She was sure recognition passed over Mara's eyes, but the witch-worker shook her head, smiling as she replied, "I don't think so."

Normally, Alice would never have pushed, but nothing was normal since she'd discovered Magic Row. She asked, "Didn't you used to live in Urbana Gardens?"

Vestra was the one who answered. Flinging an arm around Mara, she said, "She did." Vestra leaned toward Alice, whispering, "Mara doesn't like to talk about it. It wasn't a good time for her."

Mara cast her eyes down on the floor so that strands of purple fell in her eyes. When she looked up, a fake cheer replaced whatever real emotion had stirred—for the briefest second—underneath. She said, "We'd better get started with that inventory."

"Please do," said Celeste, adding, "It's the box by the front door with the police inventory for their auction next week."

"Police inventory?" Mara knitted her eyebrows.

Alice did, too. "You hold a police inventory auction in your thrift shop?"

"Magical items can't exactly be sold in a precinct," Celeste replied. "Could you two get the starting prices set today, please?"

Vestra perked up. She let go of Mara and cradled Naveed in both arms, "OK. Mind if I take the cat? You'll help me, won't you, Fluffy?"

"He'd be happy to," Alice said.

Naveed glowered. It was a wonder he hadn't transformed and threatened Vestra by now. Perhaps he couldn't disobey Alice's request for him to "blend in." If Vestra hadn't been listening, she would have reminded him that he was the one who had chosen to be a cat.

Vestra scratched Naveed behind the ears. "Hear that, Fluffy? You're coming with me. Nice to meet you, Alice, and thanks!" Vestra said.

Mara smiled, "Yeah, nice to meet you. Um, Celeste, mind if I leave early today? I'm not feeling well."

Celeste waved a hand, "Fine. Now, give me a moment with Alice, please." She added, "Thank you!" and closed the door before Mara could say anything else.

Celeste took a seat beside a small round table and

patted the chair. Alice didn't need any magical talents to see Celeste was worried. She felt her heart drop as she sat and waited for whatever bad news Celeste had to share.

"It's best not to throw the name Adelcraft around. I looked it up, you see, and it's…well, are you sure you're not a witch?" Celeste asked.

"Magic would've come in handy, but no. I'm about as Untalented as they come." It was true. Alice hadn't even had déjà vu, much less seen a ghost, gotten a hint of a premonition, or had any strokes of good luck.

"What about your parents? Did they have any magical talents?"

"I, uh…I don't know. Why? What's so special about 'Adelcraft?'"

"The kinds of Talented people come in a hierarchy. There are four basic levels: trainees, apprentices, journeymen, masters. Most witches earn these levels in their families or friend circles—there's no school for it but there are learning centers. And there's an aptitude test that determines magical talents, a lot like determining college entry. That's around the age when witches and wizards can go to one of the few training centers out there for people like us. From there, they can learn to be a level five witch or wizard, also known as a Caster of spells, a level six Binder, a level seven Weaver, and so on. But the highest level, ten, a creator of spells, only a few witches and wizards ever get that far. Adelcraft is the last name of one of the few creators in history. It's older than the Merlin line and thought to have gone extinct."

"Extinct," Alice repeated to herself.

"Alice." Celeste leaned closer. "I thought we'd have a hard time with you being human. But if you're a descendant of a creator, you'll be targeted for a whole different reason: power."

"But I don't have any," Alice said.

"You have, possibly, the blood of a creator in your veins. And blood magic is still used among some witches and wizards. Best you keep your identity hidden."

"I wrote my last name in Ron's book," Alice said.

Celeste said, "The Knights are supposed to be protectors of high-ranking wizards, so I think you're safe there. I didn't recognize your name at first, so Ron probably won't either." To Alice's surprise, Celeste laughed, "And we were worried he'd think you were Untalented."

Alice laughed, too, at the irony she should become a target for being both a powerful witch and an Untalented person. Adding to incredulity of the situation, Alice now possessed a jinn, which she had only been able to control because Mr. Kinjo had searched for one all his life.

"What about Naveed?" Alice asked.

"Daria's jinn? Are you sure Daria wasn't going to give the lamp to you all along?" Celeste asked.

"No, I—I've never seen her before…before I found her yesterday. Naveed said she was bringing him here."

Celeste waved a hand. "That was an empty threat Daria liked to use when he was being difficult. Usually, a jinn-keeper trades a jinn off to another jinn-keeper or at least someone trained in how to deal with them. Jinn are not something you just sell in a shop."

"Maybe she was giving it to you personally?" Alice asked.

"Oh, no. I'm not qualified. The only other jinn-keeper in town is Sebastian Delvaux, and he already has enough on his plate being a landlord and council member to take on another responsibility."

Before last night, Alice never would have thought a person would ever shun a genie. Who wouldn't want an all-powerful, wish-granting spirit in their corner, right? But having met Naveed last night, she understood.

"But don't you have other lamps in here? I saw a bunch on the shelves," Alice asked.

"Those are just oil lamps. They can have magical purposes, but I assure you they don't hold any spirits. Unless—" Celeste sat up, sliding to the edge of her chair.

"What?" Alice asked.

"The shelf that shook this morning, it was the one that holds the lamps. But I was sure it was the Willow kids trying to steal from me."

"Do they steal often?"

"They sneak in all the time, those shoplifters. Their mom does her best, but she's a single fortune-teller whose magical talent has been failing her lately. She's only able to make out half a vision and, even though she hasn't been wrong, she's not giving beneficial information to her customers."

"Talent can fail?"

"If we're stressed, sometimes. Between Liza's husband leaving, her kids acting out, and Hazel showing no magical talent, she's got a lot of worries. Their father is Untalented, you know. Hazel seems to have inherited his lack of magic. Zade has enough for two, and he's putting it to use, causing mischief down the street. He's getting almost as bad as Puck."

"Puck?" Alice's mind went back to her ninth-grade language arts class and Shakespeare's *Midsummer Night's Dream*. Her only reference point to the name was the wily trickster loyal to the king and queen of fairies. Come to think of it, she'd already met an "Oberon." Alice snickered, "Let me guess: his mother is named Titania?"

Celeste looked confused a second, then the corners of her eyes crinkled as she smiled, saying, "Oh, I get it. Yes, we do have a Titania in our community, Oberon's sister. Their parents were fans of Shakespeare—who was not a wizard, though many believe his words showed a supernatural talent for spell writing. But Puck isn't related to the Knights. He's either an orphan or a runaway. No one has been able to track his parents down, and he's told so many stories no one would believe him if he ever told the truth one day."

"So, Puck is a street urchin who steals?"

"Steals smartly. He's aptly named, that's for sure. Trickster, he'll talk an Untalented out of his wallet and slip into spelled places to relieve the Talented out of their supplies. Ron can never seem to pin him down."

"Then how do you know it's him?"

"If you met him, you'd know."

"Just like that? He's beyond saving, I guess, right?"

Celeste was sweet enough. But it angered Alice how

she could pre-judge teens as troublemakers, not worth saving.

Celeste studied Alice's face, picking up on the tension. She sighed, "Believe me, I wish someone, anyone, would get through to these kids, especially the Willows. But if any of the kids is beyond saving, it would be Puck Morgan. I wouldn't be surprised if Ron's theory pans out."

"What theory?"

"Daria's purse was missing. She was known to carry more than one magical item of value. Puck might not have meant to kill her, but…" Celeste shrugged.

"You can't be serious," Alice said.

Celeste cast her eyes down. "Look, I hope Ron's wrong, but I've tried, everyone on this street has tried to break through to Puck. I just don't think it's possible anymore." She looked at Alice, "I'm afraid he might have crossed the line."

Alice felt anger stirring inside of her. She hadn't even met Puck, and she knew Celeste might be right about a street urchin kid who steals for a living, but "troublemaker" to "murderer" was a long way to go. And she hated how people assumed it was as easy to jump into a life of crime as it was to make the leap in logic from "poor kid" to "criminal."

"I have another theory." Alice said, "What about a woman named Qadira Cassel?"

"I don't know anyone by that name."

"She's average height, a light-complexion, and a thin face with sharp features. I think she might be Persian or

Middle Eastern for sure. Was she in your store yesterday?"

"Sorry. We're the only magical thrift shop within three cities, so we get a lot of customers. Only the locals are familiar to me. Why?"

"Qadira came into Many Treasures yesterday asking about a lamp."

"No, there wasn't anyone…wait, yes. There was a woman in here like that yesterday—faux fur coat and glasses?" Alice nodded. Celeste went on, "She was talking about a lamp."

"She was?" Alice perked up.

"Yes, but I'm not the one who talked to her. That was Vestra."

"You don't mind if I talk to her?"

"I don't mind, but you might. Once you get her started on a conversation, you won't be able to get her to stop."

Alice didn't have a chance to ask anything of Vestra. A woman's shrill cry sounded out in the shop. Alice and Celeste jumped to their feet. Through the closed office door, the sound was muffled, but once Celeste waved it open with a hand, Vestra's screams burst in.

She was shouting, "Help!"

## 8

## PUCK, THE PICKPOCKET

"That fiend!" Vestra cried, holding her hands to her head.

Celeste ran to her side, asking, "What happened?"

"Puck!" Vestra pointed at the store entrance.

Alice looked at the swinging glass door in time to see Naveed race four-legged out through it. On the east side of the storefront glass, a boy in an orange sweater ran out of sight. Blurred out of sight, was more like it. With his magically enhanced speed, there was no way for Alice to catch him. But without thinking, she joined the chase anyway.

"Hey!" Alice shouted.

Puck not only moved out of focus but seemed to be disappearing through a wall between A Witch's Thrift Shop and Familiars Pet Store. Showing great agility as a cat, Naveed pounced. His claws dug into Puck's back so the boy screeched before being pushed to the ground. Naveed pinned him against the pavement.

Puck tried to get up. Naveed growled, his cat-like

appearance incongruous to his tiger-like roar. Holding his hands up, Puck shouted, "OK, OK, I'm down!"

Between breaths, Alice managed to say, "You're Puck?"

She remembered him from yesterday. He was the tall, lanky teen who had warned Hazel and Zade to run when Alice found Daria's body. His round, green eyes had been filled with concern for his friends. Now they were wide with fear. Alice supposed a full-grown mobster would have been afraid with a jinn-cat baring his teeth so close to the nose.

"Wha—What's wrong with Hex?" Puck asked.

"That's not Hex. Down, kitty," Alice said.

Naveed took "down" to mean he should squat on Puck's chest. His black eyes challenged Alice. He knew that wasn't what she meant. Not unlike a real cat, he just wanted to be difficult about it.

Alice might not have much experience with cats, but she was getting the hang of handling a jinn. She narrowed her eyes right back, "Off. Now." She added his name, Naveed, in her mind to cinch her power over him. He gave a throaty growl but hopped off Puck's chest as she wished.

Puck scrambled to his feet and looked between Naveed and the empty road behind him.

"You can run, but he'll only chase you down again. And he might be angrier about it next time," Alice said.

Puck took another second to think about it, then decided against running. He also changed his mind about the fearful expression. Transforming fear to fury, Puck crossed his arms. "What do you want?"

"We could start with the bundle in your hands." Alice reached for it.

Puck gripped it tighter. "I'll return it to the store. I don't have to give it to you."

Putting her hands up, Alice smiled, "Doesn't matter to me, as long as it gets to its rightful owners."

"Its rightful owners threw it away."

"They put it in a thrift shop, not a dumpster," Alice said.

"That thrift shop *is* a dumpster. It's all just people's junk anyway."

Alice crossed her arms to match Puck's demeanor. She was shorter than him, but he seemed to shrink when she said, "You know, you're not as tough as your reputation."

"Tougher than—"

"Me? Yeah, I've heard that before. Let's see, next you'll say something about how I don't know you, and how no one's ever caught you before, and all the while you're trying to figure out how you can run, which really isn't all that tough, is it?"

"Who are you?" Puck asked.

Alice adjusted her glasses, which had slid down in the run. She tried to do so in a suave sort of way, two fingers gently on the edge of her frames. She looked down as she spoke. If ever she'd wished for anything, it would be perfect control of her emotions right now.

"I'm someone who has known a lot of kids like you," Alice said.

Puck's grip on the bag in his hands tightened until his knuckles turned white. "You don't know me."

Alice grinned. "Told you you'd say that, didn't I?"

He scoffed, "So what?"

"So, I might not know you personally, but I do know what it's like to be on your own so young. Having no one looking after you, or sticking up for you, it makes you feel like you're always going to be alone, so you have to be tough."

"Like you know anything about that."

"I do. I'm an orphan, too. I grew up—not on the streets exactly—but without parents. I lost my dad when I was a toddler and when I was seven there was a fire—"

"Puck Morgan. I should have known," Ron Knight appeared as if by magic. "What's this?" He grabbed the sack from Puck's hands.

Opening the drawstring, Ron's eyes widened. He pulled out a can of gold spray paint and a brass oil lamp. It was the same one Alice had felt drawn to yesterday. *But what was the gold spray paint about?* Alice thought back to Qadira Cassel.

"Did Qadira offer a reward for Daria's lamp?" Alice asked.

Puck didn't answer. Ron was busy performing some kind of spell on the lamp. Alice didn't need magic to tell her what was going on.

She began, "He's trying to pass the lamp off as "

"A magic-stealing spell?" Ron held the lamp up to Puck's face, saying, "You absorbed Daria's jinn. That's the same as murder in the eyes of the law!"

Alice might have been unfamiliar with magic law, but murder she understood. "He killed the jinn in that lamp?"

Celeste said there was no jinn in the lamps on her shelves. But there was something about this lamp. Alice had been drawn to the brass lamp when she first entered A Witch's Thrift Shop. She had the same feeling now as she stared at the lamp in Ron's hands. It didn't seem any different from when she'd seen it yesterday morning. Which meant the jinn had been killed before Puck got to it.

Or not. Alice wasn't a witch. How could she be sensing jinn magic—or any other kind—at all? Maybe her mind was playing tricks on her. Or maybe it was precisely because she was Untalented that whatever spell had been cast on the lamp was affecting her.

"Ron!" Vestra came running down the sidewalk, "I told you he was trying to steal the lamp. He nearly killed me, hexing that lamp through the glass. It would've flown right into my head if I hadn't ducked!"

"It went nowhere near you!" Puck retorted.

Ron grabbed Puck's wrists. The silver cuffs shimmered as they locked in place all on their own. "This time you've gone too far, Puck. I'm arresting you on suspicion of the death of Ms. Daria Jinni and her jinn."

"What?" Puck exclaimed. "I was nowhere near Daria. I don't have the kind of magic to steal jinn powers. I was just gonna paint that one gold and collect the 500 bucks from that Persian lady. I swear!"

"Tell it to the judge," Ron said.

"Ron, that's a huge leap of logic," Alice tried, but her argument went unheard.

Ron launched into "You have the right to remain silent..."

And Puck did remain silent, letting Ron push him down the street toward the police car. Puck looked back directly at Alice as Ron took him away. Alice knew that look. She'd seen it before. It was defeat.

Kids like Puck sometimes had advocates in the foster system trying to help them rise above their circumstances, but sometimes there was no one looking out for them. No one was going to stand up for Puck or care enough to prove his innocence. If Puck was going to be saved from this injustice, Alice would have to find the real murderer herself.

## 9

## WEALTHY WITCHES AND WIZARDS

Not a minute after Alice and Celeste returned to the shop, as Vestra remained outside flirting with Ron, Alice caught sight of the culprit of the attack on her hair the day before. She couldn't help turning around to watch Vestra dangle her cleavage in a strategic assault on Ron's senses. She was mid-turn when the water-splashing, black limousine rolled into a parking spot parallel to A Witch's Thrift Shop.

Naveed and Celeste walked inside. Alice following them in, then stared out the window. Glared, was more like the right word, as the thirty-something raven-haired man removed his cape and handed it to the driver who had opened his door. He looked as smug as ever, head held high, chin up, and his slender, oval face lengthened with the hint of a grimace. He eyed the shop as if he smelled something foul from inside. Turning quickly before he could spot her in the window, Alice hurried to the cash register, where Celeste was placing new bills into the drawer.

"I think you have a visitor," Alice said. Naveed jumped to the counter and cozied up to the cash-register.

Celeste froze. Then, shutting the register with a bang—and ignoring Naveed's disgruntled hiss—she said, "Oh, by the moon! He's not supposed to be here until next Tuesday."

"Who is he?"

"Baz. Sebastian Delvaux, looking for his rent."

"He comes in person to collect it?" It struck Alice as a little mob-like, as if he enjoyed the power he had over people.

"Not unless you've missed a month's payment. Or three. I've made a few partial payments, but it's hard. I have a meeting to renegotiate the lease later this week."

They watched Baz's limo driver open the front door, not just for him, but for Vestra, who was coming up the sidewalk. Like a gentleman, Baz allowed the lady to go first. She blushed at him, winked at the driver, and practically skipped inside.

Alice felt a hand wrap around her elbow. Celeste leaned inches from her ear, whispering, "He's also a level nine wizard, with a spot on the International Board of Mages, so don't let him catch on to your…uniqueness here."

"I'll say he's unique," Vestra said, smiling as he approached. "Have you met him yet, Alice?"

Celeste cleared her throat sharply. "Don't you have inventory to do? Mara's never priced items for a police auction before, so go help her."

"On it," Vestra said. Naveed nearly clawed the

counter as Vestra picked him up again. He bared his teeth at Alice all the way until Vestra turned the aisle.

Alice's gaze was fixed on the gentleman in the black coat and business suit. Baz made his way to the counter as if he owned the place, which he did, Alice supposed. Still, he didn't have to be so arrogant about it.

With his back ramrod straight and a cane—or was it a wand?—gripped tightly in his left hand, he might have been a count or a nobleman. Baz was tall and lean, with his coat tailored perfectly enough for Alice to imagine he was tone beneath the fabric. When he reached Alice at the counter, he had an almost vampiric effect on her.

Ice blue, his eyes sent a chill through Alice, followed by a warmth that gripped her chest in a way she couldn't quite explain. He wasn't even looking at Alice. Celeste didn't shrink under his gaze, but she did put her hands up in surrender.

"I'll have your rent paid in full, but you need to give me until Tuesday like we agreed," she said.

"I'm not here about that." Baz removed his gloves and continued, "Hex tells me Daria was killed yesterday. Knight informs me I am a suspect."

Alice swallowed, her throat suddenly dry. What did he mean Hex told him about Daria? Was she a human he'd turned into a cat? Alice had the feeling if he knew it was her who suspected him, he might turn her into something worse.

"I'm not sure what to say. I didn't see anything," Celeste lied.

Baz said, "Perhaps it's best you didn't. May we speak in private?"

An alarm bell rang in Alice's mind. *Perhaps it's best you didn't?* That sounded like a threat. She shouldn't let Celeste go with him.

Alice spoke up, "I'm the one who found Daria's— Ms. Jinni's—body."

Now that Baz's eyes found hers, she was almost entranced by his gaze. They were not just blue as ice; they were sharp and cutting like crystals. Silver specs danced within them.

Baz tilted his head, studying Alice before asking, "Where have I seen you before?"

Some part of her brain answered defiantly, *"From drenching me with rainwater, thank you very much!"* What came out of her mouth was far too passive for her personality. She held out a hand, "I'm Alice. I work at Many Treasures, the antique shop across the street."

Rather than taking her hand, Baz gripped her chin and looked into her eyes. She felt something. Something wasn't right. Her thinking clouded until she saw only his blue eyes, such mesmerizing blue. They danced like swirling waves rushing over a deep, blue sea—

His hand jerked back. It had been yanked away by Celeste, who was holding his wrist now. Alice blinked a few times before her senses returned enough to see and hear properly.

"What gives you the right to perform a mind spell on her?" Celeste was scolding.

Baz replied, "Many Treasures is not a part of Magic Row."

"What does it matter if it is or is not?" Celeste put an arm on Alice's shoulder.

Baz said, "I would think it would be obvious to you. She is not one of us."

"I am," Alice said, coming out of her daze. She didn't know what propelled her to say it, or why she'd go against Celeste's advice when she was trying so hard to protect her. But now that she wasn't under a spell, Alice was angry, and the words flew out of her mouth: "I am an Adelcraft."

Celeste closed her eyes and pinched the bridge of her nose. Baz took a step back. Alice gained immense satisfaction from the way his mouth reshaped itself into a gaping hole. His eyes traced her frame, reexamining her. Whatever he saw in Alice, it was enough to make him rethink his approach. An apology would have been nice, but his thinking obviously didn't stretch too far from himself.

"And you think I killed Daria Jinni? Or are you in the habit of accusing people without reason?"

"Your limo was in the area around the time of her death. That's all I know and all I reported. Surely you don't have a problem with me telling the truth about what I saw?" Alice said.

Baz replied, "You don't know what you saw. I own nearly every shop on this street. I am often in this area."

"Racing away from the scene of a crime?" Alice said, referring to his drive-and-splash yesterday.

Baz smiled. "Ah, now I remember you. My driver splashed you, didn't he? I had felt bad about that, but since you are a witch, I suppose it doesn't matter. I'm sure you used a spell to dry yourself?"

"Naturally," Alice lied.

"Well, I apologize anyway. Perhaps now you can let go of any hard feelings and take back your ridiculous accusation about me being responsible for Miss Jinni's death."

Vestra's voice came from their right, "Oh, didn't you hear? Ron caught the killer. It was Puck Morgan. Can you believe it? Of course, I can. I always said that kid was—"

"Vestra, please," Celeste said.

"I don't think he did it," Alice chimed in, staring at Baz with pointed surety.

Baz didn't bat an eye. He said, "If you must have an explanation: I was late for an appointment with the board of Mages. It's public record, in a database locked with a Mage-Eyes-Only spell, so I'm sure you can find it."

Alice didn't know where her confidence was coming from at this point—maybe nowhere. Except that she was growing to dislike this "Baz" character. With enough steam to puff up her chest, she said, "I will. While I'm at it, I might look up your employee, Qadira Cassel."

Baz's eyes narrowed, "What about her?"

"She came in to see me, asking about a gold oil-lamp. You wouldn't know anything about that, would you?"

His lips pursed as if he might argue, but all he said was, "Excuse me."

Baz turned on his polished, black heels and hastened to the door. His dutiful chauffeur had both the shop door and that of the limousine open with a single snap of his fingers. Baz was just as quickly on his way, disap-

pearing from the store and reappearing behind the
darkly tinted window on the passenger seat door.

Vestra sighed as she watched him go. "He's so handsome, like a prince." Vestra put a hand on her chin and
leaned on the counter.

"You think everyone is handsome." Celeste sounded
annoyed, and not just at Vestra.

"Alice agrees with me, don't you?" Vestra asked.

Alice frowned, thinking more about Celeste's disap-
proval than Vestra's love-interests, "Well, I wouldn't say
he's prince charming."

If she wasn't so angry, she might admit he was handsome. And despite everything, she had felt something
when he'd looked at her with his deep blue eyes staring
into her soul, captivating her. But that had been some
kind of enchantment that made her feel…whatever it
was she had felt.

She wasn't attracted to Baz. He was intriguing at
best. Whatever spell he'd cast on her had played with
her emotions, and that made her angry. She could never
look dreamily at him the way Vestra was watching his
limo through the window.

"Can you imagine being with someone like him?
Did you know he's building a castle? Oh, to be the lucky
woman to marry him. A castle!" Vestra looked at her
ring finger in a starry-eyed daydream.

Celeste grunted, saying, "He wouldn't look at you
twice. Not that you're not gorgeous, Vestra, but he
wouldn't consider anyone less than a spell weaver—
much less an apprentice—date-worthy."

"You're not a master?" Alice asked, thankful her skin

was warm-toned enough not to redden as she realized how rude that must have been to ask such a question.

Vestra didn't seem to notice. She was too focused on Celeste's criticism. "I wouldn't be so sure. After all, Titania is only a master level mage, and I hear Baz is interested in marrying her."

"The Knights and Delvauxs have an understanding. It wouldn't surprise me if Baz's uncle and Titania's father were arranging a marriage for them." Celeste waved a hand to the front window, and the electric "Open" sign lit a bright red.

Vestra said, "Well, they are. And Titania's all for it. Ron told me on our date last night."

Celeste and Alice both stared at Vestra in silent wonder, for different reasons. For Alice, it was the stark realization—and disappointment—that, of course, someone as handsome as Oberon Knight would be dating someone as voluptuous as Vestra Elstar. Even their names fit together in their uniqueness.

Celeste had a different take. "Oh, Vestra. You promised. I've seen you broken-hearted too many times before to get mixed up with someone like Ron."

Vestra gave an *"I'm not listening"* eye-roll. She turned to Alice. "Celeste thinks Ron is a player who is only going to break my heart."

"He is," Celeste said matter-of-factly.

Alice really didn't want to get involved, but Vestra was determined to reel her into the conversation, saying, "What she doesn't realize is I have broken quite a few hearts myself."

Celeste snorted, "Yes, your own. More times than I

can count. It's not healthy. You are way too emotional to see when a relationship is doomed from the start."

"I am not." Vestra's brow furrowed, and her eyes reddened. Alice might have said something then, but Naveed chose that moment to jump onto the counter. Vestra ignored the cat-jinn, storming off before any tears could fall. Celeste frowned as Vestra disappeared behind the shelves.

Glancing at Alice, she said, "I don't get into all my employees' personal business like this. Vestra wears her heart on her sleeve, and her mother's track record doesn't give her the best example to follow. I'm just trying to look out for her."

Alice said, "Maybe you should tell her that."

Celeste nodded, "And you shouldn't have told Baz who you are, but I suppose you wrote it into Ron's notepad, so it might have gotten back to Baz anyway. Like it or not, that means you have to be one of us now. You'll have a lot more visits from Magic Row in Many Treasures, and a lot more scrutiny. And you might need a jinn on your side to fake your way through it," Celeste said.

Naveed looked at Celeste, then Alice, and back. Celeste pet his head, understanding some unspoken feeling Alice imagined was disdain. Naveed purred as Celeste scratched his ears.

Speaking to the cat-jinn, Celeste said, "And you, give her a chance, will you? I think this one has spunk, if not magic. Besides, if she doesn't keep you, you go to Baz or worse."

Naveed hissed.

"To Baz?" Alice asked. Of course, it made logical sense. Alice just didn't picture him and Naveed getting along. And Naveed didn't seem to like the idea any more than she did.

"Being a level nine makes Baz the highest-ranking mage in Urbana—aside from his personal tutor."

"Tutor? For a man his age?" Alice felt a smirk returning to the corners of her lips.

Celeste was not amused. "He's getting personal training from a level ten. And I don't even want to tell you who that is, since the little information I gave you seems to have overloaded your brain. You already challenged a level nine. Who knows what you'll say to a level ten?"

"I'm sorry. I was angry, and I wasn't thinking. But you said yourself: Baz might have found out my name anyway."

"What's in a name?" Celeste quoted a Shakespearean quatrain, changing the last line to a warning for Alice: "An Untalented with any other name would be in danger on this street."

## 10

## PASTS AND BEDTIMES

Celeste's words stuck with Alice the whole way home. She didn't bother keeping up with Naveed, who circled back several times and meowed to keep her going. With her hands in her pocket, she walked in a daze, considering everything. Baz, Puck, Ron, the whole of Magic Row weighed on her mind, slowing her feet on the pavement and all the way up the steps of her building.

Inside the apartment, Naveed transformed into his burly, bluish-gray genie form. He looked at her curiously. Something in his eyes had changed.

"What? Don't look at me like that. I don't want anyone feeling sorry for me," Alice started.

Naveed walked toward her—too close. Even though Alice knew he couldn't hurt her, she stepped back.

"What are you doing?" she asked.

"Alice," Naveed said—his voice was breathy—"I was wrong not to see it before, but you are talented. Maybe not the way they are, but in your own way. You are unique." He touched her hair.

Alice raised her eyebrows, skeptically, "Unique?"

"Yes. You heard Celeste. We need each other if you're to pretend to be a witch. And with me, you'll be even more powerful than a mere witch. Why, you and I... I think we may have been destined to be together." His hand slid around her waist.

"You really don't want to go to Baz, do you?" Alice asked.

Naveed placed a finger on her lips, "It's not that. Don't you see? I want to be with you." He went in for the kill, dipping her so that she was encircled in his arms. He inched his way to her lips.

Alice pulled back. "Are you trying to seduce me?"

Naveed wiggled his eyebrows, whispering, "Isn't that obvious?"

"Ridiculously obvious, Don Juan. You smell like wet fur, by the way. Have you ever done this before?"

Naveed dropped her. She tried to grab the couch to keep from falling to the floor. Ignoring her exclamation of "Ugh!" as she pulled herself back to standing, Naveed crossed his arms.

"I find humans repulsive, so no, I've never tried to seduce one before. I can't say I liked it. Look, you can solve the whole problem—yours, and mine—if you would simply say a few magic words. Even for an Untalented human, you could manage it."

Alice hefted herself back to standing. "Manage what? What words do you want me to say?"

His voice was sweet and melodic as he said in a

perfect mimic of her voice, "Naveed, I release you forever from my control."

Alice laughed. "If you want a woman to say that, seducing her isn't your best strategy. But if you really want to part ways soon, I think we can manage that."

He seemed genuinely enticed by her this time. "How?"

"If we solve Daria's murder, then I'll know who to trust, and we can work on getting you to the right people. Considering what you just tried to pull, I think it's your turn to tell me about yourself. I know nothing about you or Daria."

"All the better—"

"You sound like the big bad wolf…"

"—for you not to know. You ought not to get involved in magic affairs. I can't promise to keep you safe if you're mixed up with witches and wizards and have no magic of your own to protect yourself."

"You heard Celeste; I may not have a choice to stay out of magical affairs. But Qadira was looking for your lamp, and Puck was trying to replicate it to sell to her. I'm sure Baz sent her, which means he may have killed Daria specifically for your lamp."

"You mean humans are squabbling for power? I'm shocked."

"Be serious. If it was just about power, then why kill Daria now? Was she new to Magic Row? Did she just recently inherit your lamp from another jinn-keeper?"

Naveed sat on the sofa chair, arms crossed and one leg draped over an armrest. "She and I have lived in Merlin's Shadow for a decade or two."

"In Merlin's shadow," Alice repeated. "What does that mean? She was emulating Merlin, following his footsteps?"

"It was the name of her apartment complex. It was nicer than this one, by the way."

As Naveed examined the drapes, Alice put a hand to her chin, "Merlin's Shadow? I haven't heard of it."

"Like you had not heard of Magic Row?"

"Point taken. OK, so you and she lived for a decade or two in a magical apartment complex hidden from Untalented eyes. And you hid from the other mages, too? Blended in? Got along with everyone?"

"There were those who knew. I was, I think you'd call it an 'open secret.' Daria did not let me go out much, though."

"So, you spent most of your time in the lamp?"

"No, in her apartment. I had my own room. It was spacious—luxurious even." He looked over his shoulder at the door beside the living room.

Alice said, "That's my room, and it's off-limits. Focus. Who knew about you?"

"Many knew Daria was a jinn-keeper, even if they never saw me. But Rhys visited often."

"Rhys?"

"Rhys Merlin. He built and owns Merlin's Shadow, so he likes to visit with the residents."

"Merlin? As in—"

"As in a descendant of the Merlin line."

Alice wouldn't have believed it yesterday. Today, she realized she not only could—she did. "Is Rhys Merlin the level ten wizard training Sebastian Delvaux?"

"Yes. And yes, I have met Baz and his jinn before."

"Sebastian's, er, Baz's jinn?"

"She takes a cat form now and refuses to see me."

"Wait. Hex is a jinn? A jinn who knows you—who saved you from Daria's killer?"

"I doubt that. She hates me. We haven't spoken in a decade."

He'd said "decade" so many times, Alice was beginning to wonder if he knew how many years it meant. Maybe time was nothing to a jinn. Maybe they were immortal and had no reason to count in human years. However long Hex and he hadn't been speaking, it was obvious the female cat-jinn still wanted to protect him.

"Hex brought you to me. Which means either she disobeyed Baz, or he's not the culprit," Alice said.

"Jinn can disobey their masters if instructions are not clear or if we haven't been given instructions one way or another. We can find a way out of our orders."

"You did that often, didn't you? Is that why Daria threatened to take you to the thrift shop?"

"She was never serious until recently. She never ordered me into the lamp until yesterday."

"And you don't know why?"

Naveed shrugged, "Perhaps she'd grown tired of me. Does it matter?"

It was strange to Alice, that such dark, inhuman eyes could be so expressive. The harder he tried to act like he didn't care, the more Naveed's eyes betrayed him—as if the red lines around his pupils were the cracks in his façade. Alice almost felt bad pushing him, but she had to try. For his sake as much as hers, she needed to figure out who might still be after Naveed's lamp.

"It might give us a lead," Alice said.

"Follow your lead, then. It's not my concern. If there's nothing else you require, I'll return to my prison." Naveed meant the term "prison" to be jarring.

Alice knew it was manipulation, but fell for it anyway. She said, "No, uh, you don't have to do that. That is, you're not used to staying cooped up in the lamp. You may stay here."

Alice immediately regretted letting her emotions sway her. Her gut was telling her Naveed was going to cause nothing but trouble let loose in the apartment. She added some ground rules. "Just don't try to touch the lamp. Don't leave the apartment. And do not under any circumstances enter my room."

"Is this to be my area of confinement?" He pointed to the sofa.

"Um, well, you can use the kitchen to make yourself anything you want to eat —do you eat? Anyway, the kitchen and living room are fine as long as you don't use anything in here against me or to free yourself. Sorry, Naveed, but I can't just let you go free."

"It's gracious of you to allow me a space in your residence, however much duller it is than Daria's."

"Well, I do have some things that a mage might not have. Like this." She held up the remote for the tiny flat-screen TV sitting on a low entertainment table on the opposite wall. She'd saved up to purchase both a year ago, so the set was still nice and new-looking. "Now, don't freak out, OK? This is called a TV set, and it shows images of people." Lifting the remote, Alice pressed a button.

Naveed's eyes widened. His jaw dropped as he exclaimed, "You've trapped more jinn inside a box!"

Alice said, "No, no, they're not jinn. They're just actors and—you're messing with me, aren't you?"

Naveed snatched the remote and flipped through it like a pro. "I have seen a TV before. Daria's was bigger."

Alice threw a pillow at his head, which he caught without looking. As she stalked off to her bedroom, Naveed called out, "And I'll need a blanket!"

## 11

## MERLIN'S SHADOW

Alice liked Naveed better as a cat-jinn. He was even cute as he stalked his way down Main Street. All the way to First Avenue his ears twitched, and he glanced back and forth, jumping over garbage cans, and ducking his head down low before darting past alleyways. Alice had no trouble keeping up since he stopped and circled back three times to survey the area.

"No one is following us," Alice said on his fourth roundabout.

Naveed glanced at her. Then, as if to prove a point, he hissed at a gray short-hair who had been stalking a pigeon three feet away in front of a Chinese restaurant. The cat scrambled off, and Naveed resumed his journey, chest puffed proudly as he walked.

Alice said, "Bravo, you've cleared the way for us. But you're taking twice as long to get there, so unless you want us to be seen, I suggest you pick up the pace."

Naveed slowed—if that was possible—until he stopped altogether on the other side of the Chinese place. Standing in an alley between The Peking Palace and Urbana First Bank & Trust, Naveed looked back at her as if to say, "You hurry it up."

"Four a.m. is too early to play games like this," Alice began and ended her scolding there.

Merlin's Shadow loomed over their heads. It was a giant building, casting shadows rather than being lost to any of the surrounding buildings. Yet, when Alice backed out of the alley, it was gone. She checked twice, just to make sure.

So, there was more than one place in Urbana hidden from view. Magic Row and now Merlin's Shadow were additions to Alice's city. Was the whole world like this, with secret buildings and streets tucked away in alleys and corners where non-magical people would pass them by? Were there whole towns like that?

Naveed meowed. Twitching his cat ears, he strolled forward, leaving Alice to her gawk. She probably did look foolish, stepping onto and off of the sidewalk as if dancing with an invisible partner. What no Untalented human could see was the building that kept vanishing and reappearing, depending on where she stood. Alice couldn't believe her eyes until she'd seen it thrice.

Having convinced herself that this place, just like Magic Row, did exist, Alice stepped forward. Naveed trotted up the stoop and waited while Alice buzzed in. Since Naveed had never been allowed out of the building, so he was only guessing that the passcode and the apartment number were one and the same. Alice pressed the number he'd given her. She balled her hands into fists in her coat pockets as she waited for the door to unlock or for a mage to hex her for trying.

The click finally came, followed by the door swinging open. Alice stepped back so as not to be hit in the chin. The elderly man on the other side stopped.

"Woah, didn't see you there. You all right?" the old man asked.

Alice chuckled nervously. "Yeah, no worries, perfect timing, I guess."

"Are you new in the building?"

"No, I'm just cat-sitting," Alice said. The only thing she could think to do was scoop Naveed in her arms and show him off.

The old man patted his head and smiled, "Well, isn't that nice?"

"Yeah, I'm just returning, uh, Fluffy, to his owner, who lives here."

"Oh? I haven't seen this guy before. Who does he belong to?"

Alice had to be the worst detective in the history of crime investigation. She should have thought of a cover story in case she ran into anyone. But who was up and out the door before five a.m. anyway?

"It's a new tenant. You wouldn't know her," Alice said.

The man scratched his beard. "That's funny, I'm sure I know every tenant here, and I can't think of anyone who just moved in."

Alice's grip on Naveed tightened so that he yelped and leaped from her arms to the floor.

"I can't lose him, sorry!" Alice darted forward. She

hadn't planned to escape like that, but it worked. Alice and Naveed were down the hall and on the elevator before the man could respond. Catching her breath, Alice said, "That was close."

Naveed licked his paw and glared.

Alice shrugged. "I did say sorry."

On the fourth floor, the bell dinged. The elevator doors opened to a long hallway, which was lit and pleasant, with welcome mats and wall art and even a few tables and chairs between every fifth door or so. Naveed led Alice to room 404. She was half-expecting an error, *apartment not found,* but there it was, with an ironic rug reading "Go Away" at her feet.

*Daria has a sense of humor,* Alice thought. She looked left and right and nodded at Naveed. He touched the door with his paw and closed his eyes. Alice might have imagined it, but thought she saw a ripple in the air around the door. It traveled up to the lock.

The door opened with a click, and Naveed's slender cat-jinn body flew through it. Alice sneaked in, too. She closed the door before Naveed could transform back into his jinn form.

Calling Daria's apartment more luxurious than Alice's one-bedroom apartment was an understatement. The kitchen was an upscale black granite counter with white cabinets and a double-door, stainless-steel fridge. A white, Chesterfield sofa and a chaise faced a 50" flat screen television. Matching end tables sat on either side of the sofa. Yellow flowers bloomed on accent tables by the door and in the hallway.

Alice said, "All right, we only have a little while

before more people start waking up and going out for the day."

"There was a search spell done in here. I can sense it."

"The police?" Alice asked. If wizard officers were anything like the ordinary police, they would have done a search of her place for anything suspicious. Alice imagined it was procedure.

Naveed said, "What are we looking for?"

"Any clues as to why Daria was killed. A journal, notes, letters." Alice picked up the mail by the door. No luck there. It was all bills.

"What did Daria do for a living?" Alice asked.

"Fortune teller."

"Was she good at it?"

"Rhys once called her the best. Why?" Naveed asked.

Alice had to wonder as she saw the second notice for a late payment from the City of Urbana water services. She couldn't even begin to figure out how the City of Urbana was charging for services on a building no one in the city knew was there. Though, according to this, Daria owed them at least a month's late payment.

"Is there much demand for fortune tellers?" Alice asked.

"How would I know? I never left this apartment."

Alice put down the mail. "Where are you going?" she asked as Naveed walked to the last door down the hall.

"Daria had the same rule as you. This was the one place I could not enter."

Naveed's hand was on the knob of the bedroom at the end of the hall, but he didn't open it. Alice tapped his shoulder, pushing past him. Naveed stepped aside.

"Fine, you take this room. I'll check the rest of the home." He turned back down the hall.

Alice felt like an invader in Daria's personal space. She debated following Naveed back to the living room to search the rest of the house first. But she'd come this far.

She walked inside. The room had a bay window, a walk-in closet, a vanity, a queen-sized bed, and a dressing table. Alice went right to the table.

There was a journal resting atop a doily, but it was blank, except for a page ripped out and sticking up. It was a grocery list, so nothing interesting. Alice opened the drawers. Daria had been a fan of true crime and mystery fiction by the books she kept in there. The nightstand had no clues.

Alice moved on to the vanity mirror and desk, rifling through the drawers. While most of the contents held makeup and hair accessories, the right-most side of the desk held a jewelry box. Alice opened it to find a letter curiously tucked inside. It was still inside its envelope, with the "To" and "From" clearly legible.

"Qadira Cassel?" Alice asked aloud. Her speech brought Naveed to her. The address was Iranian. The date was November, three months ago.

"What does it say?" Naveed looked over her shoulder.

Alice read:

*"Daria, I am more than happy to come and help you with*

*your problem. I have secured a position with Sebastian Delvaux, overseeing the design of his new home. I'll take the jinn once I've settled in Urbana. If you can hold on just a while longer, I be there as soon as I've worked out the details of the design work. As you pointed out, I must make sure he does not suspect my true reasons for coming. I will be discreet.'"*

"Daria called me...her problem?" Naveed sat on the chair beside the vanity.

Alice reached her hand to his shoulder, falling short of touching. He was too unpredictable to comfort like that. She did look at him with a sympathetic smile, which lasted all of two seconds. Her attention was caught by the picture frames on the wall around the vanity mirror.

"Do you see that?" Alice pointed.

"What?"

"The picture. It's Qadira. Where is that?"

Naveed glanced at the photo. "Her home in Iran. Why?"

"Look at it. Doesn't that lamp look familiar?"

"It's a brass lamp, like the one in A Witch's Thrift Shop. You believe her jinn was the one that was killed?"

"Yeah, and maybe the killer is after you and Qadira knows it. That might be why she was so desperate to find you."

"My magic is in danger?"

"More than your magic, your life."

Naveed waved a dismissive hand. "That's the same thing to a jinn."

"Who would want to steal a jinn's powers?" Alice asked.

"The question is, who is strong enough to steal our powers? Genies have a lot of magic, which makes it hard to steal from them, but if a human were able to take magic from us, it would make them more powerful than a regular witch."

"Or wizard," Alice said, "Sebastian, Baz, I mean, is trying to become a level ten, so he's got serious magic. And he was speeding away from the scene of the crime."

Naveed stood so fast the chair flipped over. "You think he killed Daria?"

There was the anger she needed. Alice could work with that. She nodded. "He must have found out Qadira was a jinn-keeper."

"He knew she was a jinn-keeper." Naveed said. "Hex bragged that she met with jinn on every overseas visit Baz made, so I'm sure she would have met Qadira and her jinn there."

"Baz traveled to Iran?" Alice asked.

"He's been everywhere. It's part of his training as a level ten wizard," Naveed said.

Alice thought it made sense. Qadira seemed scared of Baz in her letter. Did she know he was a jinn-killer. Alice said, "Baz could be targeting jinn all over the world. And you're next."

Naveed growled something in his native tongue, and his dark eyes narrowed. "I am no ordinary jinn. *He* should fear *me*. Wish it, and I can make him regret coming after me."

Alice felt the hairs on the back of her neck rise. She was glad Naveed was her jinn and not someone else's whom she'd met in a dark alley. She shuddered. What if Daria had met a jinn like Naveed, but loyal to someone else? In the dark alley by the dumpster of Many Treasures, she might not have seen a jinn coming. She wouldn't have stood a chance against a jinn like Hex.

But if Hex had killed Daria, why would she then save Naveed by bringing his lamp to Alice? It made no sense. If there was any chance Baz was innocent, Alice couldn't allow Naveed to hurt him.

"Don't do anything," Alice said. She explained, "What we need is evidence. Qadira said I could call her. I have to see what she knows about Baz."

"Perhaps she helped him." Naveed said.

"Why would she kill Daria if she was getting the lamp anyway?"

"Perhaps she intended to double-cross Daria and sell my lamp to Baz. Daria would not have liked being fooled."

"Even if that's true, I'll only know if I face Qadira."

"You cannot face a witch, especially when she is working on that wizard's home. If he should be there—"

"As far as he knows, I'm a witch, too. And I have you."

"You would lead me straight into his hands?"

"Baz doesn't have to see you."

"Hex can sense my magic."

"Can you fight her?"

Naveed smiled. "I'm not worried about which of us is stronger. I just wouldn't want to hurt her."

Alice heard something in his voice she should have picked up on before. Naveed had strong feeling toward

Hex—the kind one might have for an ex. There could be animosity under the hurt feelings. And under hurt feelings sometimes a bit of love remail.

Alice said, "Maybe she feels the same way."

A flicker of emotion crossed Naveed's face so quickly Alice might have imagined it. Naveed asked, "And if Qadira recognizes me for what I am?"

"She's not the threat—" Alice hesitated.

Naveed frowned. That wasn't what he was asking. His dark eyes flicked down, and his jaw clenched tight, not because he was stone-hearted, but because he was hurting. Naveed felt abandoned.

Twice, if Alice let him go, too. Alice put a hand on Naveed's shoulder. And he let her.

Alice said, "Daria didn't want to give you away. She was losing her magic. But she did intend for Qadira to look after you next. I'm not a witch. I think you should go with her."

"So, you can get rid of your problem, too?" He shrugged his shoulder away.

"Naveed—"

"Let's go. Daylight's coming, and you don't want to be seen." Naveed walked to the front door and transformed into a cat.

They made it out of the building without too much suspicion. One tenant gave Alice a puzzling look. It might have been because Alice and Naveed were sticking to the walls like the spies did in action movies.

When she and Naveed were safely on the street again—in the normal, Untalented section of Urbana— Alice took out Qadira's card and walked to a payphone.

She wasn't about to give her personal number to a jinn-keeper, even if they were on the same side. Aside from that, she didn't want any witchy bystanders to overhear. Paranoia had served her well over the years, and she wasn't about to turn into a well-adjusted adult anytime soon.

Punching in the last digit, Alice was met with a "Hello?" even before the first ring.

"Hi, uh, is this Qadira Cassel?" Alice asked.

"Speaking…to Alice, I believe?"

"Yes!" Alice sounded like a rookie detective on her first case. She toned down the excitement, "I mean, yes, it is. I'm sorry to bother you, Ms. Cassel, but you said to call if I have any information on that lamp."

"Yes, Alice. I'm listening," Qadira said.

Alice took a breath. Naveed, in the booth with her in cat form, faced away, staring out of the glass at the rainy street. Alice took a breath. It had to be now, or she'd never let Naveed go. It would feel too much like abandonment.

Alice said, "I have what you're looking for. Do you think we could meet?"

## 12

## ONE WITCH'S TREASURE

**B**eing stuck all day in a shop while waiting to catch a high-ranking wizard for his crimes would be excruciating. Alice had to get out of her shift at Many Treasures this morning, but she couldn't explain the situation to Eric or she'd be putting him at risk of the same hex Alice would face if discovered. Without proof Eric wouldn't believe her anyway. She could barely explain the cat.

Eric scooped his books up and backed away from the counter. "Not again. Didn't you take that furball back to its owner on Friday?"

Alice held the door with one hand, waved Naveed inside with the other. In his cat form, he jumped onto the counter as if on the prowl, eyeing Eric like a target. Armed with his armful of books, Eric's eyed Naveed warily.

Alice set her bag down between them. "Fluffy here is a different cat than the one you saw yesterday, and he's going to be in my care for the day, so..." Alice kept her tone sharp, hoping Naveed and Eric would both take it as a warning to play nice.

"Can't you get a cat-sitter or something? I can't spend the day sneezing."

"If you let me have the day off, you won't have to waste the study-time dealing with your allergies."

"No, just dealing with customers. I've got an exam tomorrow."

"You always have an exam. I've got a life and death problem here. Look, I'll owe you, Eric, but I've got to take the day off."

Eric set down his books, ignored the angry stare from Naveed, and asked, "Life and death? What's wrong?"

Alice wasn't used to Eric's full concentration. It was a little disconcerting to see his brown eyes locked on her, his brows furrowed in concern. Now she knew how the physics text felt with Eric studying every line meticulously. She tried not to give away too much on her face, hoping he couldn't read her like a book.

Alice said, "OK, maybe not life or death, not mine anyway. It's just something I have to deal with ASAP. I can't tell you anything about it, but trust me when I say it's important. Have I ever asked for a day off on short notice like this before?"

"Last Thursday."

"What? I did not ask for last Thursday off," Alice said.

"You took the whole weekend when it wasn't scheduled," Eric said.

"Last Thursday? Eric, that Thursday was a month ago, and I had the flu!"

"All right, so it was life and death then. What is it now?" he asked.

"It's personal," Alice glanced at Naveed.

That wasn't a lie. Since Naveed took it personally, Alice had agreed to find Officer Knight and turn Baz in before turning Naveed over to Qadira. Besides that, it felt personal to Alice that someone was going after her jinn. Not her jinn, Daria's jinn, who, Alice just now realized, she had already started thinking of as her own.

Eric slid his books back into place. "Just don't make a habit out of it."

"Thanks, Eric," Alice said, picking up her purse and heading to the door. Then, because she knew it was dangerous, reckless, and more than a little stupid to accuse a high-ranking wizard of murder, she turned back around. Eric was the closest thing she had to a brother. Mrs. Kinjo called Alice *yaa ninju*, a member of the family. She could lose her memory of Eric and Mrs. Kinjo, and they'd never know what happened to her.

"If…if I don't see you, you know, the rest of the weekend, then…take care of yourself, and your grandmother, too."

Eric stopped reading. His eyes widened, and he looked up at Alice. "You got that museum job? Are you trying to tell me you're quitting?"

"What?" Alice hadn't even thought about the museum job. She hadn't told him about rescheduling the interview. But it was true that if she was offered the job, she would have to quit this one.

Eric knew that. So, why did he seem so surprised at the idea? Was it because of her sentimental tone or… Alice let the door go and stepped back inside.

"You didn't think I'd get the job, did you?" Alice asked.

"No. I mean, no, of course, I thought you might get the job. Would get the job—I just haven't looked at hiring anyone and…" Eric shrugged, "I got used to you being here."

Alice put a hand on her hip. Naveed shook his feline head; even he knew Eric was digging himself in deep.

Eric put his hands out, "It's fine. Don't worry, I'll hire someone else."

"What a relief to know I can be replaced," Alice said.

"You cannot be replaced." Mrs. Kinjo's thick Okinawan accent floated downstairs. The cane hit the stairs next, followed by the frail-limbed body of the old woman. Eric walked over to offer his help.

"Baa-baa," he began.

Mrs. Kinjo pulled the cane away, "I'm not an invalid, mago. Let me do it." Past the final step, she turned toward Alice and, surprisingly, focused on the black cat, Naveed. "Kurumayaa," Mrs. Kinjo said, translating immediately to English, "Black cat. I've seen you before. Tell me, where is my friend?"

"What are you talking about, Haamee?" Alice asked.

The fact that Mrs. Kinjo allowed Alice to call her "grandmother" in Okinawan when her grandson called her by the Japanese term "Baa-Baa" was something Alice always considered an honor.

Eric had learned Japanese from his mother and only a scattered Okinawan word here and there from his father. Though Mrs. Kinjo communicated mostly in Japanese and English since coming to America, she still considered Okinawan a sacred language to her.

Slipping into her mother tongue again, Mrs. Kinjo said, "Anuhyaa, rascal. Tell me where she is."

"Who, Baa-Baa?" Eric asked.

Mrs. Kinjo said, "My friend, Daria Jinni."

"You knew Daria?" It was almost a whisper as the revelation escaped Alice's lips.

Alice felt Naveed's fur close to her leg, his tail wrapping around her ankle. Now Alice why Daria had looked familiar. Alice had seen her visiting with Mrs. Kinjo before. She'd assumed Daria was just another of Mrs. Kinjo's friends from the bingo hall and hadn't paid close attention to her name. *Did Mrs. Kinjo know Daria was a witch?* It was doubtful, or Mrs. Kinjo would have known how close she was to a genuine jinn.

Mrs. Kinjo explained, "She came to speak to me about the lamp I received in the mail. My husband's friend, a professor in Iran, said he found a brass oil-lamp containing a jinn. I don't think he believed it himself, but he knew how my husband longed to find a jinn. So, he sent the lamp to us."

"Was there a jinn inside?" Alice asked.

Eric rolled his eyes like *"of course not,"* earning him a tap on the shin from Mrs. Kinjo's cane. Alice smiled as

Eric jumped back to avoid her swing. Mrs. Kinjo walked forward.

"There was no jinn when I rubbed the lamp. But my friend Daria knows about such things. She came here to see it," Mrs. Kinjo said.

"And what did she say when she saw it?" Alice asked.

"The jinn had been eaten."

"Eaten?" Alice asked.

Eric chuckled. "That's bound to cause indigestion."

"Mago, if you're going to poke fun at your grandfather's legacy, better you should go upstairs and make tea."

"Yes, Baa-Baa." Eric, ever the obedient grandson, dropped the smile from his face. He bowed his head and disappeared upstairs.

Mrs. Kinjo held out her hand. Taking hold, Alice was surprised at the strength to which Mrs. Kinjo clung to her. Leaning close, Mrs. Kinjo said, "There is magic in this city. People all around who have it."

"You've seen it?" Alice asked.

"Not with my own eyes, but in my heart. Yes. I know it's here. Daria had it. I could sense it in her. I told her so. Now I feel something else." Mrs. Kinjo looked at the cat, her voice breaking, "Where is she, Kurumayaa?"

Because he was in cat form, Naveed could not answer. He looked at Alice, eyes round and glistening. For a giant of a man, he was a heart-wrenching pussycat.

Alice shook her head. She couldn't let Naveed speak. Mrs. Kinjo was not a witch and didn't know about Magic Row. Alice wouldn't risk telling her. She might let it slip that she knew and put herself in danger with the magic community, too.

Alice said, "Haamee, this is not the black cat you've seen around, but I do know what happened to your friend. You should sit down."

Mrs. Kinjo squeezed Alice's hand. "She's dead, isn't she?"

"How do you know that?" Alice said.

Mrs. Kinjo let go of her hand and said, "Sometimes I feel things. I felt it yesterday morning. It was like the world went still. No wind, no air."

Alice looked at Naveed. As if he was just as puzzled, he quirked his head. *Was Mrs. Kinjo Talented?*

Alice asked, "Did you sense what happened?"

"No. I only feel things. And I felt that the lamp was a bad omen. I should not have let her take it."

"Daria took the lamp? Where was she taking it?"

"'To find answers,' she told me."

Alice's heart sank. Daria might have tried to confront Sebastian Delvaux about the jinn he'd killed. She should have had the foresight to see Baz would kill her, too.

Mrs. Kinjo asked, "Did she get her answers?" When Naveed did not respond, Mrs. Kinjo looked at Alice, explaining, "The other cat is smarter. Sometimes she nods her head, so I know she understands me."

Alice could read annoyance on Naveed's face. Any second now, he'd talk and give Mrs. Kinjo a heart-attack. Alice swooped past him, leading Mrs. Kinjo back to the staircase.

Alice said, "Everything is going to be all right,

Haamee. Eric should have your tea by now. Tell him to come back downstairs when he's done."

"Such a good girl." Mrs. Kinjo tapped her hand started up the steps. Midway up the steps, she stopped and asked, "Are you leaving us?"

Alice shook her head. "Never," was the answer that jumped immediately to her lips. At that moment, she meant it so much her eyes watered.

In a solitary part of her brain she chose not to acknowledge, Alice recognized certain qualities about herself. She was defensive, sarcastic, and guarded. With Eric, with her college friends who inevitably dropped out of her life for it, and even with Naveed, she never showed deep emotions. Vulnerability was not a skill she possessed—even though she tried. With Mrs. Kinjo, though, it was like Alice was a well, and the old woman had her own rope and bucket. Maybe bringing out emotions in Alice was Mrs. Kinjo's magical talent.

It was more likely just how love worked. Puck didn't have anyone who loved him like that. The only person who might have loved Naveed like that was dead. Alice seemed to be the only one in a position to help both Naveed and Daria Jinni get justice. So, she kept true to her promise, Alice headed out the second Eric returned.

Outside, Alice and Naveed headed toward the police station. Ron was the only wizard officer Alice knew, but now that she knew there were wizard policemen, she would be looking for signs of magic among those behind the badge. Alice wasn't sure if she was supposed to feel safer or not with witches and wizards on the force, but there didn't seem to be any animosity toward the Untalented—except they wiped the memories of any Untalented who knew they existed.

Then there was the jab in labeling non-wizards "Untalented." Couldn't the mages call non-magical people "regulars" or "normals" or even "non-mages?" Alice mused on that as she walked past the bus stop. Then she backtracked as she heard her name.

"It is Alice, right?" It was a kid's voice.

Alice looked at a bench where two kids and a gentleman in a suit were waiting for the bus. The way the man's shiny, black shoes were pointed away from the kids and he concentrated on his newspaper said he wasn't with the teens. Plus, Alice was sure the Willow kids hadn't been there a second ago.

"Zade and Hazel," she acknowledge them each in turn.

"You are a big fraud," Zade said.

Alice's chest tightened. "Pardon?"

The man glanced at Alice and turned his body sideways, concentrating on his paper. Pretending not to listen was more likely. He hadn't given a sign of noticing the twins appearing out of nowhere, and they gave no sign of noticing the man's discomfort at their raised voices.

"You said you'd help Puck, but you won't," Zade said.

"How do you know I'd help Puck?" Alice asked.

Hazel and Zade looked at each other. Then, Hazel said, "Celeste told our mom."

"They're friends?"

"They both work on Magic Row. They talk," Zade said.

"Shh," Alice said, then she realized the man couldn't have overheard the words "Magic Row" or any other part of their conversation. The kids had made themselves invisible, so from the man's perspective, Alice was talking to herself.

The man, who wasn't listening, raised the newspaper higher. Alice gestured with her index finger for the kids to follow her. A few steps away from the bus stop, the man wasn't able to throw sideways stares at the crazy woman talking to no one.

Naveed refused to follow, possibly because he was too busy casting disconcerting glances right back at the Untalented gentleman. The man scooted until he was half-off the bench, but Alice couldn't bring herself to care about his discomfort. She focused on the kids.

"Why would you think I'm not going to help Puck?"

Zade raised his voice. "Because you're just like everyone else, living it up in Merlin's Shadow. No one in that ivory tower cares about us."

In a more level-headed tone, Hazel said, "Because everyone who promises they'll help him turn his life around gives up. Our mom said it herself."

Now Alice understood. For kids with parents, the parents sometimes warned about the ones without. It wasn't always unfounded.

"This time is different. I'm not trying to change Puck's life, only he can do that. But I know he didn't do anything more than steal a lamp from the thrift shop.

He didn't kill anyone, and he shouldn't go to jail for something he didn't do."

"You're really going to help him?" Hazel asked.

These kids were cynical for such a young age. Alice thought she remembered the strength of teenage emotions but, even without parents, she'd never been this distrusting; the Kinjo's may have been to thank for that—they were always kind and, more than that, honest with her. Alice tried that now.

"I don't live in Merlin's tower, I went there to check out Daria's apartment. I'm not '*going* to help' Puck because I already am."

Hazel and Zade were silent for a moment. Then, Zade asked, "What can we do?"

The sound of squeaky brakes and clattering doors alerted Alice to the arrival of the morning bus. The man in the dress suit was handing the driver his pass. Alice pointed.

"You can catch your ride," she said.

Hazel shook her head, "That's not our ride."

"Officer Ron was going to drop us off at a Talented Teens program."

"Community service." Zade's tone was grudging.

"And he said to meet him at the bus stop?" Alice asked.

Zade lifted a chain out from under his shirt; it had a medallion with the same type of writing on it as on Hex's collar. "Untalented people don't notice us unless they're concentrating really hard. It's like we're invisible. It would look weird if Officer Ron started talking to himself in the station."

Alice understood that. The man in the suit was still spooked. He stared out the window at the black-eyed Naveed as if he was the devil in a cat-suit. Come to think of it, Naveed was scary enough in his jinn form that Alice could see the resemblance.

"You work on Magic Row, don't you? Didn't Delvaux give you one of these?" Hazel pointed at her brother's medallion.

"Yeah, guess I forgot it at home," Alice said. "Look, can you tell Officer Ron I need to talk to him as soon as he's done dropping the two of you off?"

"You're on to something, aren't you? What is it?" Hazel asked.

Alice hesitated. "Let's just say the lamp Puck took was already emptied before it arrived in Urbana. I'll tell the rest to Ron when he meets me. Tell him he can find me at the building site of Sebastian Delvaux's new home."

"As long as you're helping Puck, you got it," Zade said.

Alice smiled. It was good to see Puck had people who cared about him. Alice counted herself on that list as she and Naveed boarded the bus. Qadira had said to come by anytime, that she'd be working at the building site of Baz's mansion. It was risky. Then again, Alice figured there would be workers there, and even a rich and powerful wizard like Baz wasn't likely to attack either one of them around witnesses—especially because rich and powerful men had the most to lose. If he did attack, Ron would hopefully be there in time to catch him. Then he wouldn't have to take her word for it that he was Daria's killer. Alice felt like a hero.

There had been a lot of kids she couldn't help when she was growing up, but she could put things right for Puck, Hazel, and Zade. And Alice wanted justice for Daria, the woman with whom she shared a special bond in the cat-jinn who was taking up more than his half of the seat. All Alice needed was one final clue to the killer's identity. Somewhere up the hill, on a street called Enchanted Avenue, she would find it.

## 13

## CASTLE AND ROOKED

1 37 Enchanted Avenue was not obscured by magic. Visible to all, the street and home might have been pleasant if not for the looming clouds and threatening rain. The building-site wasn't the castle Alice had pictured, but rather a modern-day mansion with castle-like features.

Alice and Naveed admired the landscaping as they traversed down a long, U-shaped driveway, rows of juniper trees and azalea bushes guiding the way. Around a bend was a fountain, not functioning yet, and full of windswept leaves. A set of steps led to oversized double doors made of solid wood, varnished and polished so fine Alice could almost see her own reflection. Like a castle, the mansion was made of gray stone with pointed towers that reminded Alice of a witch's hat.

The west side was not yet completed. In its place was a structure of steel beams, waiting to be made into walls. A hanging scaffold shook in the wind with a foreboding knock, knock, knock against the skeleton of the building.

Alice echoed the sound with the door knocker shaped like a cat's paw.

One of the double doors creaked open, seemingly of its own accord. Alice clutched her chest as a woman's voice croaked, "Alice?" Qadira appeared to her left. Magic was the only explanation as to how she had opened the door without holding the knob.

"Qadira? I wasn't expecting you to open the door yourself." Alice was pleased with how confident her voice sounded.

Qadira beckoned her inside with a hand wave, her eyes fixed on Naveed as she said, "I had to send everyone else away due to the prediction of a storm today. It's fortuitous."

"How so?"

"Some of the construction team are not mages, so I usually send them home when there's magic to be done. In this case, even wizards are not privy to seeing jinn magic."

"Is there actually going to be any jinn magic on display? I thought I was just giving you the lamp?"

Naveed was at Alice's ankle again. She could feel the hairs rising on his body and felt the same with the hairs on the back of her neck. Something seemed wrong.

"I have to command the lamp and take control of the jinn inside." Qadira said, leading Alice into a completed living room with a fireplace, large enough to stand in, gently crackling to her right. To the left, thin plastic sheets separated them from the incomplete tower. The sheets swayed like ghosts, and the wind whistled through them with an "oohing" sound, sending shivers down Alice's spine.

It could only have been magic that partitioned the complete and incomplete parts of the mansion so definitely. Sawdust sat under the swaying plastic, but the chairs and fireplace were spotless. More than that, the room felt warm—so much so Alice felt heat rise to her cheeks.

Qadira spoke again. "Transfers of power are much better done when the previous owner is present. It is a shame that Daria was killed before we could even meet. There was so much she could have told me to make the transition easier on both the jinn and myself."

Qadira reached a table where a doily sat—clean, white, and waiting. She set the tips of her fingers on it, and Alice understood she was asking her to place the lamp in the center. Naveed curled his tail around Alice's leg as if holding her back. She hesitated.

Qadira's brow furled. "What is it?"

The way Alice's brain worked was a lot like the city she lived in. There were roads of logic she traveled often, ones she rarely went down, and ones that, much like Magic Row and Merlin's Shadow, she didn't always acknowledge existed. Right now, logic was placing a sign in front of her reading *"Danger Ahead."*

Qadira seemed so friendly. Alice couldn't see why she should be scared. Paranoia, that was all that was stopping her.

Opening her purse, Alice took out the lamp. Her brain tried again, sending a slight tremor to her hands. Alice clutched the lamp.

"Is something wrong?" Qadira asked.

Alice's brain pumped blood to her ears with the pounding warning, *"Don't speak!"* She swallowed down her fear and spoke anyway.

"Where were you Friday morning?" Alice asked.

Qadira's eyebrows raised. "I beg your pardon?"

"The morning Daria was killed, where were you?"

"I was here, working," Qadira said.

"You didn't visit Magic Row?"

Qadira's hands moved to her hips. "Is there a point to these questions?"

"Just a few hours after the murder Friday, you were in my shop, looking for this." Alice raised the lamp very slightly, Qadira's eyes followed.

"I was supposed to meet Daria on my lunch break," Qadira said. "When she didn't show, I went to do some shopping. Then, I found out she was dead. I'm sure you can understand why it was a priority to find the lamp after that."

Qadira walked a few paces back, to a stool by a construction table. Sitting, she gestured to another stool beside her. Alice didn't budge.

Qadira said, "Alice, I understand your fear, and I know this place can feel spooky. A half-finished castle is not my first choice for a jinn exchange, either. I want to get the transfer over because I'm afraid whoever attacked Daria might be after you even now."

"Aren't you afraid they'll be after you if you take it?" Alice asked.

"I'm leaving soon enough, and even if I stayed,

anyone would be a fool to try going up against me. I'm trained in the protection and keeping of a jinn."

"So was Daria," Alice said.

"My cousin was getting old. She was starting to develop dementia, and her fortune-telling suffered for it. She was having a problem paying her bills, and she was fired from Reading and Co. She tried to appeal to Mr. Reading, the owner, and the landlord, Sebastian Delvaux. I promised to help her work out some way to keep living in her building and to take the jinn since she cared for him so deeply and wanted to make sure he wouldn't fall into the wrong hands. She asked me here to help, not to hurt her."

Alice looked at Naveed, whose head hung low. At least now he knew Daria's *"problem"* referred to dementia and unemployment, not to him. Daria had cared about Naveed, so deeply that she asked her cousin to look after him when she was no longer able.

"I didn't know Daria was your cousin. I'm sorry for your loss," Alice said.

Qadira's eyes teared as she said, "Daria was my first cousin on my mother's side. She was the one who taught me how to be a jinn-keeper. I...I'm hurt and angry she's gone."

Alice did not budge from her spot near the fireplace, but her voice softened. "Who do you think killed her?"

"I don't know the people here well enough to accuse anyone. I am as uncertain of you as you are of me, but for the sake of the jinn, I had to take a chance and meet you. Will you bring the lamp to me, please?"

Alice hesitated. Qadira seemed genuine. She was not

forcing the lamp away from Alice and, alone in this house, she had plenty of opportunities to kill Alice and steal the lamp. Though she might have heard the rumor about Alice's last name, and the thought that Alice was a tenth level mage or even related to one might have been what was holding Qadira back.

But then, Daria had written to Qadira, asking her to come to Urbana. If she had intended to give her the lamp all along, she wouldn't have had a motive to kill Daria. *Wasn't giving her the lamp the right thing to do?* Cautiously, Alice placed the lamp on the doily.

Qadira stood. "May I?" She asked, glancing between the lamp and Alice.

Alice nodded. The tightness in her stomach relaxed. Qadira approached. She did not try to snatch the lamp or to put up a spell to keep Alice away. Instead, she smiled, and her hands hovered around either side of the golden lamp.

Naveed, still disguised as a cat, wrapped his tail tighter around Alice's ankle. Alice bent down and picked him up. She wanted to whisper to him that it was all right, he would be fine, but the closer Qadira's hands came to the lamp, the more a lump rose in Alice's throat.

It was strange she should be so emotional about losing Naveed. She'd only known him two days, and he had given her grief almost the whole time. Still, she found herself clutching him tightly and not wanting to let go. It struck her then that Qadira had lost another jinn just like Naveed recently.

Alice said, "I'm sorry about your other loss, too."

Qadira glanced up. "What?"

"Your jinn. Whoever killed Daria took all the magic out of your jinn first, in your home country. Didn't they?"

Hands suspended an inch from the lamp, Qadira froze. Seconds passed before she lifted her hands to her cheeks as if wiping away an invisible tear.

"That's right. It's difficult for me to talk about," Qadira said.

The look on her face wasn't genuine pain, or hurt. Suddenly, Alice wasn't sure she saw tears earlier. She wasn't sure Qadira was telling her the truth. Alice couldn't give Naveed away while she still had the slightest bit of doubt.

"It might be difficult to protect this jinn, too. I think he'll be better off under police protection." Alice reached out to take the lamp back.

Qadira brought her hands down like a barrier between Alice and the oil lamp. Through a forced smile, Qadira said, "This one is more powerful than my last. He'll be fine with me." Her fingers gripped the handle.

A man's voice came from outside. "Stop there, Qadira."

Alice breathed a sigh of relief. It was about time Ron got here. The plastic sheets parted, but the man stepping through wasn't the hero she had been expecting.

Sebastian Delvaux, in his black suit and tie, holding his cane, or wand, like a sword, entered the room. Baz pointed the wand at Qadira and narrowed his eyes. By the man's feet, Hex hissed.

When Naveed joined in with his own growls, Alice whispered, "Shh, calm down." But she was saying it just as much to herself. Still holding Naveed, Alice stepped back, closer to the fireplace.

Qadira batted her eyelids. "Mr. Delvaux? What are you doing here?"

"Catching you," he replied.

"Me? For what?" Qadira held her hand to her heart like the accusation hurt.

Delvaux stepped closer, wedging himself between Qadira and Alice. "I had my suspicions when you wrote to me about a job, and more when Daria began losing her powers shortly after I hired you. But it wasn't until Miss Adelcraft said you had gone to her store asking for the lamp that I realized what you were after. When Miss Adelcraft suggested to Officer Knight that the lamp was emptied in Iran, I understood your true purpose in coming to Urbana."

"You think I stole the jinn's power? You were in Iran when you hired me. You're the one training to be a creator mage—the one with the skill necessary to steal a jinn's magic. It's so clear that you're trying to frame me. I don't think the mage community here will fall for it."

Baz's face contorted and his nostrils flared. He looked as if he might speak, but couldn't find the words. Qadira backed away, reaching a hand out to Alice. "You and I can fight him, Alice. If we combine our powers," Qadira said.

Baz stepped toward Alice, keeping his wand on Qadira. "Do not trust her, Miss Adelcraft. She is Daria's killer, not I. Move away from her, now."

Qadira whispered, "He is trying to separate us, so you and I will both be weak and he can kill us, as he did my cousin."

Baz's eyes narrowed. He seethed. "That is a lie."

Baz eyed the lamp. Qadira was closer. She grabbed it and disappeared. Not as in *moved very fast*, she *disappeared*. Baz pointed his wand at the tower scaffolding with a skill and agility that told Alice he was wielding real power.

Through the plastic sheets, a form could be seen high overhead on a wooden beam. Baz shot at Qadira. Sparks, like electricity, flew from the wand. She vanished in time for the blast to hit the beam instead of her. The hanging scaffold knocked violently against the metal beams of the unfinished building. Baz disappeared the same way Qadira had, and Hex ran into the construction zone. Naveed darted after, but Alice couldn't tell if he was chasing Hex or Qadira. How could she tell who was the victim and who the attacker?

If Baz was right, Qadira killed her own jinn and Daria, and now she was after Naveed. If Qadira was telling the truth, Baz was framing her and trying to steal the lamp. Alice couldn't waste time debating which was true. She had to keep Naveed safe until Ron had a chance to arrive.

Qadira re-emerged on the ground level, less than ten feet from Alice. Though her form was distorted through the plastic, Alice could hear her clearly.

"The name! The jinn's name. Alice, tell me!"

Alice shook her head, shouting back, "If Daria

wanted to give him to you, she would have told you his name!"

"She died too soon! She did not have the chan—"

A lightning-like strike hit Qadira's arm, the lamp skidded toward the plastic covering. She vanished again. Alice rushed to the lamp, lifting the sheet to snatch it off the ground.

She had the lamp again. But even while Qadira had it, she couldn't control Naveed, not fully, without knowing his name. *The name was part of the transfer ritual,* Alice realized.

Naveed had told Alice his name, but that was because he thought Daria had given him up voluntarily. Maybe Naveed didn't have to give up his name as long as Alice commanded him to keep from telling it.

That would be a clever rule to keep others from stealing jinn. There might be other ways for Qadira to find out the name, but she was busy in a magical fire-fight at the moment. And besides that, Alice had the lamp again.

But what could Alice command Naveed to do now? Attack Qadira or Baz? Freeze them until Ron got here? Was Naveed's power stronger than Baz's and Qadira's? Was Naveed more powerful than Hex? Alice wished she knew more about jinn magic. Qadira appeared behind her.

"The lamp, quick!" Qadira said.

Alice backed away, toward the tower. "No," she said, recoiling from the greediness in Qadira's eyes.

Qadira's whole expression shifted to rage. She lunged toward Alice and caught her by the hood of her jacket. Qadira's voice was low and cold as she said, "Then you can die, too."

Alice tried to run. She pulled away, but in seconds her feet were stomping on air. Suspended from the top of the unfinished towers, Alice flailed. Pure panic pumped through her arms and legs as she tried to grab onto something—anything—around her. All that was keeping her from a forty-foot fall was Qadira's hand on her jacket.

A thud on the beams jolted Qadira's footing. Alice dropped a half-foot and yelped, but Qadira kept hold. From a lower position now, Alice could see the hanging scaffold from the corner of her eye. Baz stood on the top beam across from Qadira, armed with his wand and ready to attack.

"Do not come closer!" Qadira said. She looked down at Alice. "The lamp and the name of the jinn or I swear I will make the Earth open up and swallow you!"

It was no idle threat. The ground beneath them shook, sucking a juniper into the ground below. Alice wanted to scream, throw up, or both—but fear was a vulnerability. Anger was better. She knew how to use it.

Alice lashed out the only way she could. She said, "Go ahead and drop me. See what kind of witch I am." Then Alice dropped the lamp.

Qadira screeched and let go. Alice saw her opportunity and reached to catch the hanging scaffold. Her hand just barely caught a rail, and the scaffold swung. Paint buckets slid her way. Alice began to slip.

Above, a cat growled. Alice could hear, but not see,

Qadira struggling with a feline attacker and finally shouting, "Get off of me!"

Alice had no time to feel glad. As her sweaty palms gave way, she whispered, "Naveed, help me."

Then, she fell. As if from nowhere, a tail wrapped around her wrist and tugged. Alice grabbed the scaffold again, this time pulling herself up and over the rails. Once safely inside, she panted.

"You could have used a little more magic," Alice said between breaths. "So I wouldn't have had to climb so much."

Naveed didn't give a hiss, or make any reaction. Instead, he looked up as a loud meow sounded above. Alice understood now that it had been Hex, not Naveed, who had attacked Qadira. The two cat-jinns had strategized this—saving Alice and distracting Qadira at the same time.

Baz delivered the final blow. Flashes of light followed in short succession. The full-on wand-fire was met with a gust of wind so powerful it knocked Baz's wand out of his hand and tilted the scaffold. Things were not going to plan.

Alice grabbed for the railing so she wouldn't plunge forward. Naveed's tail wrapped around her foot and he swung this way and that, dodging paint buckets. Brown and tan paint splattered to the ground, where a crack in the earth was swelling, threatening to swallow everything that fell into it, including the scaffold itself. The ropes snapped.

"Naveed, the lamp!" Alice said. She'd thrown it deliberately onto the scaffold. Now it tumbled through the air. What would happen to Naveed if his lamp sank deep into the Earth? She didn't want to find out.

The fur at Alice's ankle was replaced by strong arms at her waist. In his jinn form again, Naveed flung Alice high into the air. She landed with a thud on the beam directly below Qadira and Baz. Naveed continued to fly toward the lamp.

Only when she was safely on the tower beam, did Alice realize what she'd done. If Qadira got the lamp, she would have rights to the jinn of the lamp, and now she knew his name, completing her control of him. If Naveed took possession of his own lamp, which Alice had ordered him to do, then he became his own master. What would he be like as a free jinn, who seemed to hate humanity? Would he become a villain worse than Qadira? Alice couldn't take the chance. She could not undo her order, but she could clarify it.

She whispered, "Into the lamp, Naveed."

She heard him curse as he disappeared in a puff of jinn smoke.

Qadira caught the lamp. "Your cat was the jinn? How clever!" She cackled.

Alice was horrified. Then she noticed Hex, lying on the beam three feet from her. Alice crawled forward. Hex winced, her gold eyes trying to focus on Alice.

"Are you all right?" Alice scooped her into her arms.

The ground shook, and Alice gripped Hex tightly in one hand and grabbed a vertical beam with the other. So close to the edge, Alice could see a glint of gold rising from the ground.

Alice looked above, careful not to let Qadira see her.

If Qadira thought Alice had fallen, that gave Alice an advantage. But the lamp was all the advantage a skilled witch needed, and it was rising to the air, toward Qadira's outstretched hands.

Baz's voice rose to a shout. "That jinn is too powerful, even for you. If you try to absorb him, you'll both die."

"I'll take my chances," Qadira said. Then she began chanting something in a language Alice did not recognize.

Hex lifted her head, so her collar was visible. She looked at Alice as if trying to tell her something. Alice turned the gold collar over, but there was nothing written there now. Hex scratched at the collar with her paw until it slid all the way, so the latch was visible.

"You want me to remove this?" Alice asked.

She couldn't be certain that this wasn't like freeing Naveed to reign terror on humanity. Was Hex a good-natured jinn Baz was keeping hostage or a threat to all mankind? Naveed had said he and Hex were different, and Hex seemed to be trusted by Mrs. Kinjo and the mages of Magic Row.

Hex looked up, prompting Alice to do the same. The day was gray and bleak, but the darkness directly overhead was unnatural. Baz's magic flew in chaotic sparks, but every time the smoke cleared enough for Alice to see Qadira, it the cloud around her thickened again. And the darkness grew.

Hex's yellow eyes pleaded with Alice.

"I hope I'm doing the right thing," Alice whispered.

She unlatched the collar. Hex disappeared. Alice,

still clutching the collar in one hand, gripped the beam as the dark clouds to her level.

Even as Baz cleared the fog and advanced, Qadira laughed. But her laughter died in her throat. "Wha— what is happening?" Qadira asked.

Alice held onto the skeleton tower and leaned to catch a glimpse above. The darkness cleared enough for Alice to see Qadira pale. Her skin gave off an unnatural glow. Baz disappeared and reappeared just feet away from Qadira, with his wand now in hand.

"No," Qadira scratched at her throat. Then her hands dropped, and her voice changed. She said, "I relinquish control of the lamp. The jinn known as Naveed belongs to you, Alice."

Qadira met Alice's eyes with a smile and deliberately dropped the lamp. Some words in a strange language followed, then Qadira closed her eyes and her body shook, as if the spirit possessing her had leapt out.

*Hex possessed Qadira long enough to break her control of the lamp.*

Alice caught the oil lamp by the handle. She rubbed, ready to do what she should have done in the first place. In a burst of black smoke, Naveed appeared.

Above, Qadira snapped out of her trance. "No! Where is the lamp?"

"My goodness, Qadira," Baz said. "Whatever possessed you to use such an ancient spell?"

"What spell?" Qadira asked.

Baz said, "Relinquishing your powers as a jinn keeper."

From her position on the lower beam, Alice could

see only enough of Qadira's face to watch her expression shift from shock, to fear, to rage in a span of seconds. Qadira's voice grew shrill and twisted into something monstrous as she lashed out. "I still have more power than you!"

Two beams of light met above. Qadira's bright red against Baz's blue. In seconds the red was overtaking the other.

"I must help," Naveed said.

Alice nodded, "Stop her."

## 14

## HEROES AND VILLAINS

Naveed left Alice by the main support beam, watching the battle from below. Like a magical tug of war, Baz's beam of blue magic gained the advantage, then Qadira's, then Baz's again, and so on until Qadira's red energy nearly overtook Baz completely.

Naveed reappeared high over the beam of clashing light, where neither Qadira nor Baz could see him. He moved so fast Alice was amazed her eyes could follow the movements. She couldn't explain it, but part of her knew that if she wasn't holding the lamp, she wouldn't have seen Naveed as anything more than a blur.

Naveed grew in size, then zoomed toward the energy and wrapped a massive hand around whole of the beam. He gripped the sum of Qadira's and Baz's magic like it was solid, a lightning bolt in his hands, which he threw back at Qadira. It struck her in the heart. Baz lifted his wand, suspending fire.

"No!" Qadira grasped her chest.

Naveed disappeared and reappeared behind Alice.

He held his hands forward, aiming at Qadira. A cocoon of magic burst from his hands. Purple, black, and blue, depending on the angle, the tar-like substance wrapped around Qadira's wrists and ankles, then the whole of her body. She wriggled, trying to break free.

"I will not die like this!" Qadira shouted before the cocoon sealed over her face.

"Don't kill her," Alice said, panic rising up in her chest.

Naveed said, "Calm yourself. Baz cast a power-stripping spell, but Qadira's was meant to kill. She *would have died* if I hadn't cocooned her in complete safety."

"So, nothing can kill her while she's wrapped up like that?" Alice asked.

Naveed said, "She'll be fine until a medical mage can heal her."

Baz walked forward, pushing Qadira back with one hand so she fell to the ground and rolled into the crater she'd created. Headlights lit the construction site as Officer Oberon Knight's patrol car pulled into the driveway.

"Get me down," Alice whispered.

Naveed put a hand on her shoulder. Alice found herself back in the living room. The plastic sheets separated her from the scene, but she heard sound of Ron's door opening and shutting. Baz explained what happened, but the words were soon drowned out by the drizzle of the rain just beginning to fall.

Alice put a hand to her head. The shock and fading adrenaline would turn into a migraine soon. She hadn't expected Naveed to notice, but he took her arm and guided her toward a stool. His touch was gentle, and he surprised Alice as he asked, "Are you all right?"

"I will be," Alice feigned a smile as she sat.

Naveed turned back into a cat as Baz opened the plastic covering and stepped into the living room.

"That was some display of magic," Baz said.

Alice nodded. "If she was powerful enough to kill a jinn-keeper, she must have had a strong talent for magic."

"I meant yours."

Alice blinked sharply. It took her a moment to realize Baz's misconception. He hadn't seen Naveed—his movements had been too fast. Instead, Baz had concluded it was Alice's own magic he'd witnessed on the tower.

Baz thought she was a witch, after all. Alice was fairly sure pretending to be a witch meant not throwing up after insta-traveling. She took a deep breath, trying but not quite managing a "Thank you."

Baz sheathed his wand. "You seem to be in shock, Miss Adelcraft?"

"No, I'm fine," Alice tried her best to look it.

"In that case, may I have the collar back?" Baz reached out.

Alice was still clutching Hex's collar so tightly her knuckles were turning white. She handed it to Baz. He sank to one knee and latched the collar as if he was fastening it to an invisible cat. The second it snapped on, a cat appeared within it.

Alice swallowed back her amazement, reminder herself to act like a witch. Baz rose to his feet. Hex trotted over, walking a full circle around Alice's stool as if to say thank you. Naveed puffed his furry chest up with pride and met Hex at the end of her circle. Hex hissed and ran away, with Naveed chasing after her.

Baz said, "Ungrounding Hex was a dangerous choice, but it did give us the advantage over Qadira, so I suppose I should thank you."

Alice understood. The necklace grounded Hex to the world. Without it, she returned to the spirit world and could only exist on Earth by possessing a human— as Hex had done with Qadira. But it did beg the question of why Hex had possession of her own object of grounding.

"Hex is a free jinn, isn't she?" Alice asked.

Baz smiled. "It seems you do know something about jinn magic. Most witches think jinn are only attached to oil-lamps. Hex's necklace belongs to her—it was only right I give it back. She has proven ever since that it was the right choice. She is not a jinn with any animosity toward humans."

"But she stays in cat form?"

"That's her choice. Only a few people know she's a jinn and she likes to keep it that way."

"It must be hard." Alice couldn't imagine not only being separated from her own kind, but also having to keep being something she wasn't.

Baz said wistfully, "I don't know why she stays."

"She risked the spirit realm for you today," Alice said.

"I think she may have done that just as much for

you. I underestimated you. It seems Hex sees more in you than in other witches."

Alice blushed. Scrambling to change subjects, she said, "You said I helped you figure out Qadira was Daria's killer?"

Baz replied, "Hex keeps her eyes and ears on all the areas near Magic Row. When you told the Willow children the lamp was emptied before coming to Urbana, she took it to mean that it happened in Iran—under the care of its previous owner."

"Or because its previous owner was the one who drained the lamp, which Qadira did." Alice had come close to the same conclusion. "But," she asked, "Why kill her own jinn?"

Baz answered, "Some rare witches and wizards learn a spell allowing them to absorb a jinn's power as a way to increase their own Talent. It's a short-cut to becoming a creator mage, but it's unstable magic and folly for a human to steal it."

"Not to mention, it's murder." Alice said.

Baz nodded at that, but his eyes took on a faraway look and he pursed his lips in thoughtful silence—a look that made him surprisingly attractive. Alice cleared her throat, breaking his concentration.

"What is it?" she asked.

Baz replied, "One thing puzzles me. If Qadira did kill her jinn, why bring the lamp here?"

Alice could clarify that. She said, "Mrs. Kinjo, the owner of Many Treasures, still knows some treasure hunters who used to work with her husband. One of them in Iran sent the lamp to Many Treasures. When Mrs. Kinjo showed Daria the lamp, she put it together that Qadira was a jinn killer. She confronted Qadira and was killed for it."

"I had wondered how the lamp had gotten here. That explains the box. Though how it ended up in A Witch's Thrift Shop is still a mystery," Baz said.

Alice could explain that, too, now that she thought about it. "Celeste said that her shelves shook that morning. She thought it was Puck and the Willow kids trying to use their magic to steal, but it must have been Qadira. Your limo came around the corner quickly enough that Qadira would have had to stash it quickly. She had enough power to make it appear on a shelf a street away, didn't she? The lamps were visible from the window. She might have thought it would go unnoticed hiding in plain sight until she could go back for it. She didn't count on Puck stealing it to pass it off as Daria's jinn."

A masculine voice responded, "That's the most likely conclusion." Ron entered the room, wiping the raindrops from his hair. He turned his radio down, adding, "Qadira is being taken away as we speak. I've got two mage officers assigned to watch over her and a medical mage who works as a doctor at the hospital."

"Will Qadira recover?" Alice asked.

"Unsealing her from your magic will be tough. That's some power you have," Ron said.

Alice blushed. Naveed's magic, combined with her last name, was giving her a reputation she'd hoped to avoid. It was better than them finding out she wasn't a witch, she supposed.

"Do you need me to undo it?" she asked.

"Magic removal is a tough procedure, but our doctor is trained. Qadira will be fine until we can get her back to her home country. Mage law there will deal with her sentencing."

"Thank you, Knight. Well done." Baz and Ron shook hands.

Ron added, "You better call me Ron and I should call you Baz if we're going to be brothers-in-law."

Letting go, Baz said, in a voice struggling to sound comfortable, "Right, thank you, Ron."

"You're welcome, Baz." Ron shook his head. "That'll take some getting used to, but there it is," he said, then he took his leave.

An odd feeling rose in Alice's heart. Baz's and Titania's engagement meant nothing to Alice. Why would it? But she did feel awkward watching Ron's and Baz's exchange as they acted like this arranged marriage was a fact of life.

The adrenaline was fading now that the excitement was over. There was nothing else to do, so Alice looked around for Naveed. He walked back over to her, looking wet, angry, and annoyed. Hex must have argued with him again. Alice bent down and scooped him into her arms.

"I suppose you'll want to take Naveed?" Alice asked when she and Baz were alone again.

Baz stated the obvious, "Even if I wanted to, he and Hex don't get along." His eyes studied Alice again, this time the blue didn't seem so cold. Baz added, "You may not be a jinn-keeper, but you seem to have the skill. Do you think you can take on a jinn like Daria's? I've heard he's a handful."

"I can handle him," Alice said. At the moment, she believed that she and Naveed shared a bond. The way Naveed acted, she recognized hurt, pain, and a need to lock others out of his feelings. She often felt the same.

Even though Daria had taken care of him, she had not understood how utterly alone Naveed had felt, or she would have known that keeping him locked away from the rest of the world would only make him bitter and angrier at humanity. Maybe Alice could help him learn to see people in a better light, and he might do the same for her.

"Then good luck to you, Miss Adelcraft." Baz offered a hand. Alice slipped her petite fingers into his firm grip. He held on a second longer than was necessary. Then, he let go and walked deeper into the home.

Alice said quietly, "Naveed, time to go home."

## 15

## A WHOLE NEW WORLD

Alice loved her job at Many Treasures even more now that she knew the occasional customer was a witch or wizard in search of rare magical items that might find their way into the Kinjo's shop. This morning, a young witch and wizard stopped by for a personal reason.

"Here is a thank you from Puck, bought and paid for, not stolen." Hazel handed Alice a navy-blue collar, just the right size for Naveed in his cat-form.

The name on the silver plate read *Fluffy McScratchins.* Alice struggled to hold in her laughter. Not quite managing a straight face, she said, "It's perfect! But you didn't have to get anything. I just wanted to help keep Puck and you two out of trouble."

Zade shrugged. "We can't promise we'll stay out of trouble."

"But I promise to help you try," Alice winked. "Speaking of which, I saw a sign on Celeste's window on my way here today. It said 'Help Wanted.'"

"So?" Zade asked.

"So, I thought one of you could apply—or both if she needs the help. You're fourteen, and that's working-age in Urbana. You might be able to help your mom out."

"We know about the opening." Zade looked at his sister.

Hazel looked around before standing on her tiptoes and replying in a soft voice, "You know why they're short one worker, right?"

Alice leaned her elbows on the counter and asked with a puzzled brow, "Why?"

Zade answered, "One of the workers went missing."

"You mean she quit?"

"We mean she didn't show up for her palm-reading with mom last night and today all her stuff is gone from her apartment—everything but the furniture," Hazel said.

"We heard our mom calling Celeste this morning. They think she disappeared, just like that." Zade snapped his fingers.

"If she took her things, that's not really disappearing. That's more like leaving in a hurry," Alice said.

"That's what Celeste said when our mom said she should file a police report. She said, 'Quitting a job and moving in a day isn't a crime. Just a nuisance for the owner,'" Hazel said.

"But it's weird, right? Leaving a day after a woman is killed."

Alice didn't entirely disagree, but she reassured the

teens. "We know who killed Daria, and as far as we know, there was no accomplice."

With a quizzical brow, Zade said, "We don't think she's an accomplice. Mara was nice. She wouldn't yell at us like Celeste. She even gave us money sometimes to help us out. We think she was afraid, like she was targeted, too."

Alice doubted that, unless she was a jinn-keeper, too. From what Celeste said, there was only one of those in Urbana now, and he didn't seem to be afraid of anyone. If there was a connection between Daria and Mara, surely Celeste would have seen it.

"I'm sure it's just a coincidence. There are a lot of reasons why grown-ups up and move. I don't think you two need to worry about it."

Alice couldn't think of any good reason for a person to move suddenly, but she didn't know Mara, or anyone in the witch community well enough to jump to conspiracy theories.

"Just like every other adult." Zade moved away from the counter.

"We thought you were different," Hazel said, before following her brother to the door.

"Wait," Alice said. She knew they were guilting her into action like a script. They were probably expecting the next line. "I will look into it."

The teens smiled—a good impression of delight and surprise. They knew what they were doing, and Alice was falling for it. Except, she added with her index finger in the air, "On one condition: one of you needs to apply for the job at A Witch's Thrift Shop. And you have to stay in school on weekdays, and no more stealing."

"We said we couldn't prom—" Zade began.

Hazel elbowed him in the stomach, saying, "Done. You got Puck off the hook, I'm sure you can help Mara, too. Thanks, Miss Adelcraft."

"Oh, no. Please, just call me Alice."

"Thanks, Alice," Hazel and Zade each called out as they left. They passed by an old man who was just coming through the door. He side-stepped Zade, who said, "Oh hi, Mr. Merlin," and, "Bye," in the same sentence.

"Merlin?" Alice asked. She recognized the bearded man she'd met in the lobby of Merlin's shadow. "You're Rhys Merlin?"

The old man grinned. "And you're Alice Adelcraft, or so I'm told. You're quite the talk of Magic Row."

Alice winced. "I didn't do anything."

"Except catch a killer. It's strange, I wasn't aware an Adelcraft lived in town, except for a young woman and her child, who both died in a fire years ago."

Alice's eyes widened.

Naveed jumped out of his cat-bed onto the counter and looked between Alice and Rhys.

Alice wanted to say, "That was my mother who died! I lived." But that would be dangerous. Her parents were not witches, and to admit to her origin would reveal that to anyone who had known them.

Rhys didn't seem dangerous, though. He was a healthy-looking old man; slender, average height, and dressed a little like a hippie. He wore a beaded necklace, a brown leather jacket with fringes, and a pair of small, round, sunglasses which he'd slid to the end of his nose. Rhys seemed genuinely happy, like he had just found an old friend he hadn't seen in ages.

There was a glint in his eye as he said, "Apparently, the girl did not die, but became a powerful witch."

Brushing a lock of hair behind her ear, Alice looked down. "Did she?" she asked. She held her breath as she wondered if Rhys could see through her.

"The only thing is, the mother of this young girl was not a witch."

Alice's heart could have stopped. Was he going to tell her secret? Would he place a memory-erasing spell on her right now?

The bell dinged. Vestra bounded inside, waving hello and smiling. In a pink sweater dress with a bow on the top, she looked altogether too cheery for the end of the world. Alice's world was about to be spelled out of her memory.

Rhys smiled at Vestra, then winked at Alice, leaned forward, and whispered, "Just between us? The father was."

The father was a wizard? Alice wanted to ask, but her heart was beating so fast she needed a minute to catch up. Rhys nodded, turned, and left. Vestra said something but Alice didn't hear it.

Vestra set her elbows down on the counter with a thud, pulling Alice out of her trance. Naveed hissed and jumped back into his bed. Vestra reached out.

"Sorry, Fluffy! I didn't mean to scare you. It's just me, remember me? Of course, you do, come here!"

Naveed was pulled against his will into Vestra's arms. She stroked him and kissed the top of his head. He winced but soon relaxed into her grasp.

"What can I do for you?" Alice tried to sound like a person who hadn't just heard a life-changing revelation.

"A bunch of us were going to watch the meteor shower tonight. Thought you might like to join us?"

Before she could answer, the familiar thump, thump, thump down the stairs alerted them to Eric's presence. This time, he was juggling a pile of books and biting down on a pencil. Alice ignored his entrance. She'd seen him every day for years. But Vestra stood up, fixed her hair with her fingertips, and whispered, "Who's the guy?"

Vestra tugged on the collar of her shirt, just enough to reveal a hint of what was wrapped beneath the bow. Eric caught sight of her and reddened. She flashed him a smile and waved. It wasn't magic, but it worked just the same.

"He's not a level ten wizard, I can tell you that much," Alice said.

Vestra responded, "I don't care if he's Untalented. Think he'd be interested in the meteor shower?"

"Actually, yes," Alice said. Eric could probably show her all the constellations, and Vestra would show him their romance was written in the stars. Neither of them would have any idea what they were getting themselves into. And because of that, Alice added, "Better count me in, too."

So, it began.

Many Treasures was officially a part of Magic Row.

Alice was now a member of Urbana's magical community. She no longer needed to wish on shooting stars—she had a genie for that. And with all the vision boards she'd made, for the first time in her life, Alice could see the beginning of a bright and magical future.

## THIS IS JUST THE BEGINNING

*For those still wondering who I am, you'll have to read until the end of the series to find out. As you'll see when Alice follows the mystery of Mara Blest, there is much more story to tell. And, Alice is nowhere near making the discovery that will change her forever: me.*

## BOOK 2: BEWITCHING BARGAINS

*The story is just beginning!*
*Read about Mara's disappearance in Book 2: Bewitching Bargains.*

*For updates on new releases, visit: astoriawright.com*